# ALSO BY ALEX GINO

*Melissa*

*You Don't Know Everything, Jilly P!*

*Rick*

*Alice Austen Lived Here*

# GREEN

ALEX GINO

Scholastic Press / New York

Library of Congress Cataloging-in-Publication Data available

ISBN 978-1-338-77614-0

10 9 8 7 6 5 4 3 2 1          23 24 25 26 27

Printed in Italy 183
First edition, October 2023

Book design by Maeve Norton

For us, because we all deserve joyful communities

# ★ CHAPTER 1 ★

# SAINTLY CARROTS

Green's life was pretty great, especially for a kid in middle school. They were queer and nonbinary, and had lots of queer and trans friends. Pretty much everyone used their name and pronouns, and they felt mostly comfortable with their body the way it was. They didn't have a nemesis or a bully or anything like that, and most of their teachers were at least halfway decent, if not rather good. Their family was small, just them and Dad at home, but Dad was way closer to awesome than awful. Yep, the going was sweet for Green Gibson.

One of the best parts in Green's day was lunch with kids from the Rainbow Spectrum, Jung Middle

School's group for LGBTQIAP+ students and issues. Not that everyone from the group ate lunch together. Dini ate with the kids who practiced magic tricks, and Devon usually hung out with the other soccer players, but Green, Rick, Ronnie, Melissa, Kelly, Leila, and sometimes a few other kids could be found at the same table most days, sharing laughs and snacks.

Green was first at the table that day, pulling a peanut butter sandwich, three clementines, and a juice box out of their red reusable lunch bag, same as usual.

They wondered where Ronnie was and spotted him and his signature pink sneakers by the lunchroom cashier. He had reddish-brown hair that fell in light curls around his soft white face. Ronnie's fourth-period teacher often let the class out a little early. Most days, he got to the table before Green, especially if Green had to go to the bathroom. Green used the gender-neutral one in the nurse's office, which was out of the way, but it was also a private stall that never had a line.

"Don't you ever get bored of the same thing every day?" Ronnie asked as he plunked down a plastic tray that held a cheeseburger in a silver pouch and a pile of waterlogged carrot slices mixed with waterlogged cauliflower florets.

"I'd rather be bored of my lunch than frightened by it," Green said.

Ronnie put a white napkin over his still-wrapped burger and held it as if it were hovering in the air. "Woooooooh, I am a scary burger ghost!"

Green pointed down at the veggies. "I was referring to those. I wonder what they did to deserve that punishment."

"It looks personal. I'll bet they knew the cooks' big secret!"

"Or they had some secret the cooks were trying to get out of them!" Green mimed holding a bunch of carrots by their stalks and affected a growly, stern voice. "You will tell us all you know, or we will dump you into the boiling water, mua-ha-ha!"

Ronnie laughed. "It looks like they took their secret to the grave." He poked at his vegetables with a plastic fork before unwrapping his burger and taking a bite. "The burger's pretty good though."

"And full of vitamins," Green joked.

Ronnie shrugged.

"You want a clementine?"

"Sure."

After Green passed it over, Ronnie put it to the side of his tray. But Green knew he would eat it soon enough. Ronnie always shrugged when Green offered him a clementine, but he always ate it. That was why Green brought three: one for themself, one to share with the group, and one for Ronnie.

Green would have been happy to joke with Ronnie the whole lunch period, but then Leila, a short

Latina American girl with straight, long, jet-black hair, joined them, agreeing that the carrots and cauliflower had suffered for some great sin. Melissa, a freckle-faced white girl with a round nose and long brown hair held back with barrettes, arrived soon after, and with Melissa, of course, came her BFF Kelly, an exuberant biracial Black girl with her hair in two thick twists. Melissa sat down next to Leila, her girlfriend, and kissed her on the cheek. Green wondered what it would be like to kiss someone on the cheek when you saw them.

Kelly held out a plastic container with three parts. In one was the homemade spread, sliced pita strips filled a second, and a pile of neatly stacked carrot sticks rounded out the meal. Leila passed, but Ronnie and Green each took a carrot stick and dipped it lightly into the garlicky mixture. Melissa, who had tasted Kelly's dad's hummus before, grabbed a big scoop with a pita slice.

"Not bad," said Green.

"And these carrots must have been saints!" exclaimed Ronnie.

Green and Ronnie laughed, but the rest of the table, even Leila, who had been there for the end of the carrot consequences conversation, looked at them oddly. They high-fived, and Green could feel Ronnie's warm, soft palm against their own.

"*Ha'SNIT'inavu!*" Rick, a kid with a friendly smile who was mostly quiet except around his good friends, joined the table with a strange sneeze-like greeting that Green assumed came from *Rogue Space*, his favorite show.

"Okay, everyone's here," Kelly said, grabbing Melissa's arm. "Tell them! Tell them! Tell them!"

"Kelly!" Melissa snapped in her best friend's face with her free hand to get her attention. "Stop talking so I can tell them!"

Kelly made a sour face, but then turned to everyone and said, "Listen up! Melissa has an announcement."

Melissa couldn't help but laugh at her best friend's enthusiasm. "I was talking to Mr. Sydney this morning, and tomorrow he's *finally* going to tell us what the spring musical will be."

Mr. Sydney, who had been faculty advisor of Rainbow Spectrum last year, was back in his role as spring musical director, now that Mx. Abrams had returned from parental leave and was running Rainbow Spectrum again.

"It's the moment we've all been waiting for!" exclaimed Kelly.

"It's the moment *I've* been waiting for, anyway!" said Melissa with a grin.

"Are you gonna audition?" Green asked Melissa, trying to act like they didn't know the answer.

"Is Melissa gonna audition?" Kelly repeated the

question as if it answered itself, then answered it anyway. "It's a play! Of course she's gonna audition."

Melissa cleared her throat. "Kelly, we've talked about this."

"Right, sorry. It's Melissa's choice whether she will audition." Kelly paused briefly, then attempted a whisper. "You *are* gonna audition, right?"

Melissa revealed a giant grin. "Of course I'm gonna audition. It's *me* we're talking about." Melissa was a natural onstage, and had been since she was the surprise star of the fourth-grade play.

"So, any idea what it's gonna be?" asked Rick.

"He wouldn't tell us in class," said Ronnie. "But he said it would be a classic."

"You know *classic* just means *old*, right?" said Leila.

"That pretty much rules out anything with openly queer characters," said Melissa, wrinkling her nose.

"Well, I'm gonna be in the band, no matter what

the play is," said Kelly. "My dad said I'm gifted at the clarinet, and he's a professional musician."

"I'll probably join the crew," said Ronnie. "I love that behind-the-scenes stuff. What about you, Green? I'll bet you're a great actor."

Green wondered what they had ever done to make Ronnie think they were a great actor. Green didn't even know for themself whether they were any good. But the idea that Ronnie thought so made them feel kind of warm and funny.

When it came down to it, though, Green didn't really think of themself as an actor at all. Or a crew member. Or a clarinet player. And even if Green did want to be an actor, most musicals didn't have non-binary characters. They sighed and said, "I dunno. I agree with Melissa—*classic* sounds like it's gonna have lots of boy roles and girl roles and not a whole lot of nonbinary roles."

"I'll bet Mr. Sydney would let you try out for whatever part you wanted," said Leila. "Right, Melissa?"

Melissa shrugged. Sometimes Mr. Sydney was cool, but sometimes he wasn't as cool as he thought he was. It was like he drove a shiny convertible but he didn't realize the trunk was filled with outdated ideas.

Green picked at their clementine peel, enjoying the bright citrus scent that wafted up when they pierced it with their thumbnail. "Let's see what the play is first."

Even if Mr. Sydney let them try out for whatever part they wanted, the idea of playing a boy onstage wasn't very exciting. It was certainly less terrible than playing a girl, but in order not to have a binary gender, they'd probably have to play a rock or something.

The conversation turned to the latest season of *Candy Pirates*, an animated show about three flamboyant pirates who lived together on a ship. They were always hunting for treasure in the form of gum-drop islands, chocolate reefs, or some other sweet ocean treat. It was kind of silly, but also kind of fun, and the pop star Miss Kris voiced Green's favorite character, Peregrine the Parrot.

Green did their best impression of Peregrine's screech, and Ronnie responded with "Arrrrrrr, Polly wanna quit it?" in a perfect Percival Pirate.

Green tried not to notice how cute Ronnie was. And funny. Ronnie had never said he was queer, so Green didn't ever think they'd ever be more than friends. Which was fine. Except when Green noticed how cute and funny and friendly he was.

"*Squawk*, quitting is for losers, *squawk*," Green said back to Ronnie, quoting Peregrine.

It was true. Green's life was pretty great, but that didn't mean they had everything they wanted.

# CHAPTER II

# POP QUIZZES AND OTHER SURPRISES

Green hadn't always noticed how cute and friendly Ronnie was, and they hadn't always laughed a little too hard at things like haunted burgers. Last year, Green had mostly known him as Rick's best friend who came to Rainbow Spectrum. Green didn't have classes with either of them, and for a while, they weren't entirely sure which boy was Ronnie and which was Rick.

This year, Green and Ronnie were in the same English class. They sat together at a two-person desk five days a week, listening to Ms. Richards drone on about the genre and theme of whatever story they were reading.

Green wasn't sure at first what they thought of Ronnie, a kid who seemed to talk a whole lot about his two moms, Mama B and Mama C. But soon they were having fun chatting before class about how annoying even cool parents could be, and how weeks and weekends should be switched, so that you got five days off for every two days you went to school.

Green wouldn't have necessarily called Ronnie a friend, so much as a kid they knew. That is, until the week the class read a story about ice pickers, a group of men who climbed dangerous mountain peaks. Or at least, that was the story they had been assigned to read.

Green had meant to read it. They really had, but it was so boring that they fell asleep while trying to read the first page. Dad had suggested that they were probably just tired and should try again over breakfast, but in the morning, it was somehow even worse. Green read the same long paragraph three times before they could pay enough attention to understand that the narrator was saying it was very cold. On a snowy mountain. For an adventure story, there really wasn't a lot happening.

In class, when Ms. Richards asked about the setting of the story, Green confidently raised their hand. They knew that if they answered an easy question early, it would look like they knew what they were talking about, and they wouldn't be called on for a harder question later.

"The Himalayas!"

"Well, yes, we know that's the mountain range from the caption on the first page." Ms. Richards looked down at them from over her thin oval glasses. "But which specific peak was it?"

"Oh, I, um, uh . . ." Green wasn't used to not being able to answer a teacher's question, especially not when they had raised their hand.

"Does anyone know?" Ms. Richards's face soured as she looked around the room. "Ronnie?"

Ronnie looked at Green with panic in his eyes. "Mount Everest?" he said hopefully.

Green's heart sank in their chest on Ronnie's behalf. They didn't remember the name of the mountain, but they knew it wasn't the name of a mountain they already knew.

Ms. Richards cleared her throat in disappointment. "No, it is *not* Mount Everest or Sagarmatha, as our adventurers learn the local Nepalis call it. Does anyone know the answer?"

Dozens of pairs of eyes found specks of dirt on the floor and walls to examine.

"Hmm, I see. Well, how about the names of the characters?"

Green started searching through the story, and they weren't alone, as the room filled with the sounds of books hitting desks and papers flipping.

"Paul!" called out one kid.

"George!" called out another.

"Put your books away." Ms. Richards sighed. "In fact, clear your desks entirely, except for a clean sheet of paper and a pen."

The class groaned. A single sheet of paper was never a good sign.

"Pop quiz!" Ms. Richards announced.

The class groaned again, louder this time.

"Question number one." Ms. Richards paused for effect. "What is the name of the specific mountain the characters in this story climb?"

Green heard a few pencils writing, but they and Ronnie just shook their heads at each other.

"Question number two: What are the names of the main characters of this story?"

Green wrote down Paul and George, hoping that the students who had checked were looking at the right pages. They added Nick, which was their dad's name, and then Ronnie. They smiled when they did that, not entirely sure why it felt good to write his name down, especially when they were both in the middle of failing a pop quiz. But it did.

The next questions were even harder, asking about how one character got hurt and what they ate when they reached the summit.

Finally Ms. Richards collected the papers and announced that they would be doing a grammar lesson. She dictated sentences and glared at her students as they wrote and underlined the prepositional phrases.

Green stole looks over at Ronnie whenever they dared, and when their eyes met, Green's stomach flopped like they were on a school bus that had driven over a huge bump in the road.

Twenty boring sentences about things being *in,* *under,* and *toward* other things later, the bell rang and Ms. Richards dismissed the class with a reminder to read the story before class tomorrow, because there just might be another quiz.

Green joined the class in packing up their things, and noticed that Ronnie was moving extra slowly. His face looked like a deflated balloon.

"You okay?" they asked once they got into the hallway.

"I've never failed a test before."

"Wow." Green was pretty good at school, but they had failed more than a few spelling tests, and that science test last year when they got herbivore and carnivore mixed up.

"I'll bet your moms will be cool about it," said Green.

"Yeah, they probably will. It's more that I never

thought of myself as the kind of kid who fails tests."
Ronnie winced.

"Well," Green said with a grin. "There's always room to grow."

Ronnie wrinkled his face. "Since when is failing a test *growing*?"

"Not failing the test," said Green. "But learning that you can fail a test and still be you."

"Um, okay," said Ronnie.

"That's what my dad said when I failed my first test."

"Let's hope my moms are each at least half as cool as your dad."

"At least they'll know you didn't cheat!" Green suggested.

"Or, if I did, I'm very bad at it." Ronnie cheesed a grin, and Green laughed so loud the three kids ahead of them turned around in surprise.

It wasn't anything special. Just two kids walking down a crowded hallway, jostling between elbows and backpacks, talking about failing a quiz. But it was also everything special, because it was the moment Green knew they didn't just like Ronnie. They *like* liked Ronnie.

## ★ CHAPTER III ★

# WE'RE OFF TO SEE THE WIZARD

As promised, Mr. Sydney got a turn at the microphone during morning announcements the day after news of the audition spread at the lunch table.

"Good morning to all the potential performers out there!" he proclaimed. "I am delighted to reveal that this year's musical will be . . . *The Wizard of Oz*! Watch for signs around the school for details about auditions, which will take place a week from Tuesday."

Ms. Jones's math class exploded into a chorus of complaints. Jung Middle School had been performing *The Wizard of Oz* as far back as anyone on the staff could remember. Once the kids who had performed it when they were in sixth grade graduated, it came around again, like some sort of musical locust.

Ms. Jones waved her hands in front of her like a conductor trying to hush an orchestra. "Quiet down for the rest of the announcements. There will be time for your comments and critiques later."

She was right. All day long, the school buzzed with Oz talk. Most kids griped about the choice, but they were still excited to declare who they wanted to try out for, and who they thought would get which part.

Green didn't have much to say. *The Wizard of Oz* was definitely a play that only had parts for boys and parts for girls. One of the characters was even named the Tin *Man*.

At Rainbow Spectrum, the play was all anyone wanted to talk about. And while lots of kids planned to try out, they also had plenty to say about the choice. During check-in, Mx. Abrams had to keep reminding people that they were supposed to hold off on back-and-forth discussion until everyone had gotten a chance to speak.

"That movie is so old," said Leila.

"The books are even older," added Devon, a tall, athletic kid with wire-frame glasses and a sharp fade.

"You'd at least think we could do *Wicked*," said Melissa.

"Or *The Wiz*!" said Kelly. "The music in that one is so good!"

"I'll bet we're only doing it because we already have the costumes," said Tracey, a Black girl with a brazen attitude and a charming smile.

"My sister was Toto when she was in seventh grade," said Mika.

"My mom was Toto when *she* was in seventh grade!" said Talia.

"Well," said Mx. Abrams after check-in was done, "I guess it's clear what we're talking about today. I will say that *The Wizard of Oz* is a Jung Middle School tradition, and Tracey isn't entirely wrong about the costumes. Materials for costumes and sets can be quite pricey, and the spring musical is supposed to be a fundraiser. Every dollar the school spends on the production is a dollar that doesn't get, say, more diverse books into the school library."

Mx. Abrams's well-reasoned point was met with grumbles of acceptance.

Melissa spoke next. "Okay, so it's an old play. But they can still make sure it's a welcoming space for everyone."

Green felt a little jolt of excitement at the word *everyone*. *Everyone* included nonbinary people, especially when someone like Melissa said it.

"Right?" said Kelly. "Why does Dorothy have to be played by a girl? I mean, Melissa's gonna get the part, but otherwise, it could be a boy."

Green winced at the word *boy* and looked over

at Jay, a white nonbinary eighth grader who usually wore striped button-down shirts. They looked as uncomfortable as Green did, maybe even more. Green didn't want to be the one to have to say it, but they also wanted it said.

"It doesn't have to be a girl *or* a boy, you know," they pointed out.

"Oh, right," said Kelly. "I'm sorry. What I meant was, *anyone* can be Dorothy. Or, well, any of the other parts. Melissa's going to be Dorothy."

"Mr. Sydney would probably be quite open to hearing your concerns," said Mx. Abrams. "Though I might hold back on the casting recommendations."

"Mr. Sydney should have thought about it without us having to say something," said Leila.

"Maybe he already has?" Talia's voice rose, as if she were asking about the possibility, rather than suggesting it.

"He didn't say anything in the announcement," Mika responded.

"And don't you remember last year, when we had to teach him about the singular they?" Tracey reminded everyone. "I think we should check in."

"You're absolutely right!" Kelly shot out of her seat.

"Kelly?" asked Melissa. "Where are you going?"

"To talk to Mr. Sydney!"

"But . . . ?" Melissa prompted.

Kelly looked around her and sheepishly sat back down. "We should figure out what we want to say first?"

"That's generally how it works," said Melissa. "And?"

Kelly sighed and singsonged, "And maybe I'm not the one who should say it. Sometimes working in alliance means passing other people the mic."

"She can be taught!" said Melissa, raising both hands and shaking them in pretend amazement.

And so they spent the remainder of Rainbow Spectrum figuring out what Mx. Abrams called their aims and talking points, which was a fancy way of saying what the problem was and what they wanted Mr. Sydney to do about it. They wrote up their concerns in a letter.

Dear Mr. Sydney,

We at Rainbow Spectrum are excited for this year's spring musical. AND we want to make sure that everyone feels welcome to participate. Some of us have been in plays in the past where girls had to play girl parts and boys had to play boy parts, but not everyone wants to do that. Plus, how are nonbinary people supposed to try out? We hope that you will let everyone try out for whatever part they want, and that you will not consider their gender when you make your decisions.

Sincerely,

Rainbow Spectrum

The letter went around the circle for everyone to sign their names if they wanted to.

Green signed it, but they weren't totally happy with it. They wished it said something about how nonbinary people shouldn't have to play binary roles, and that if they really wanted a show that was inclusive, there would be nonbinary characters as well as nonbinary actors.

The letter went next to Rick, who signed and passed it to Ronnie.

Green was glad to see that Ronnie signed. They expected he would, but he hadn't actually said anything about the letter as they were writing it. Green had started to worry that maybe Ronnie thought the letter wasn't his issue to get involved with. Worse, maybe he didn't think it was all that important.

But then, when all the signatures were done, he volunteered to give the letter to Mr. Sydney in the morning, before first period. He even took out his binder to place the letter inside, so that it wouldn't get wrinkled.

Green couldn't figure him out. But that didn't stop them from wanting to.

After Rainbow Spectrum, a pack of kids headed toward the bus stop, and most of the others walked home, leaving Melissa, Kelly, Green, and Ronnie standing in front of the school. Melissa's mom pulled up for Melissa and Kelly, and soon Green and Ronnie were alone. Ronnie leaned on the stop sign at the corner, the sole of his sneaker resting along the pole.

"Don't you usually take the bus?" asked Green.

"Yeah, but it's Mama B's birthday, so Mama C's picking me up so we can go surprise her at her office."

"Oh, cool."

"Yeah, I guess. Mama B loves showing me off at work, so that'll be fun. You know the drill."

*"Oh my goodness, look at how much you've grown!"* said Green, in a gravelly, deep voice.

*"I haven't seen you since you were this big,"* said Ronnie in a high-pitched drawl. And then in his own voice, "And they hold their hands an inch apart. Even infants are taller than that. And then there's my personal favorite." Ronnie brought back his silly grown-up voice. *"Do you remember me?"*

"Right?" Green exclaimed. "You just got through telling me how I was the size of a slice of bread the last time you saw me. How am I possibly supposed to remember you?"

"And why would I remember you out of the adults there the one time I met you? Like my moms say, 'You're special, but you're not that special.'"

"Oooh," said Green, "that's good. I'm using that."

Ronnie smiled. Green smiled back. The quiet felt peaceful, the kind where you don't have to worry about what the other person is thinking. It felt that way for a full eight seconds until nerves took over and the silence felt too thick.

"So," said Ronnie, piercing the conversational fog, "are you going to try out for the play if Mr. Sydney approves our recommendation?"

"I'm not sure." Green blew at the tuft of hair that had dropped into their face. "Not if all the characters are boys and girls. I know, acting is about being someone you're not, but if I never have the option of playing someone with a gender like mine, I don't think I want to do it."

"Oh," said Ronnie, followed by a "Wow." He tilted his head and paused again, as if the thought were sliding to the rest of his brain. "Thanks for sharing that."

"Um, you're welcome, I guess." Green chuckled nervously.

Ronnie laughed. "I got that from my moms. I just mean it's good that you feel okay sharing that kind of stuff with me. I know I'm a cis het guy, and that means I need to be extra-aware when people let me in."

*A cis het guy.* It wasn't that Green thought Ronnie wasn't cisgender. And Ronnie had said at Rainbow Spectrum that he was in alliance with queer people like his moms. But Green had never heard Ronnie call himself heterosexual before. At least not for as long as they had been listening for such things. It bounced like a heavy ball in their brain.

They noticed the silence in the air and realized it was their turn to speak. "Well, I think you're doing a really good job."

"I try." Ronnie grinned.

That's when Mama C pulled up and Ronnie hopped into the car.

Green could still see Ronnie's smile when they closed their eyes. They didn't want to open them.

It was good that Ronnie knew he was a cis het guy, but Green couldn't help thinking that it would be even better if he weren't.

# ★ CHAPTER IV ★

# BIG LITTLE FAMILY

Saturday morning in the Gibson household meant pancakes. Lots of pancakes.

The weekly ritual began with Dad rattling around in the cabinets. Green's bed was on the other side of the kitchen wall, and the clang of the heavy, cast-iron skillet hitting the stove was like a Saturday alarm clock.

Green and Dad lived alone, but Dad prepared batter for eight: four adults and four kids. Lulu, who lived upstairs, would be down with her six-year-old twins, Kandy and Randey, and Lulu's girlfriend, Jan, would be over with her toddler, River. Nana usually came too. Soon, the kitchen table would be filled with pancakes, butter, maple syrup, jam, and whatever fruit Jan had brought with her. Lulu would bring down a pot of coffee and Dad would have hot water ready for Nana's tea.

By the time Green got dressed and joined Dad in the kitchen, the place already smelled like butter and there were pancakes on a tray in the oven to stay warm. The first few never rose quite right, and they didn't develop the perfect crisp edges of Dad's later batches, but the beige blobs were perfect for Kandy and Randey, who complained that Dad's deliciously browned, puffy delights were burnt.

Green set the table, and by the time they were done, Kandy and Randey had burst through the door. They were fraternal twins, but sometimes they seemed to be two copies of the same person.

"We could smell the pancakes from upstairs!" announced Kandy.

"That's how we knew it was time to come down!" added Randey proudly.

"And where is your mother?" Dad asked.

"Don't worry, she's moving," said Randey, which was how Lulu described her morning sluggishness.

"And she started the coffee!" Kandy confirmed.

They went to the window and bet on who would get there first, Jan and River or Nana.

"Jan and River always get here first," said Randey.

"Not always," countered Kandy. "I think Nana's gonna beat them today." Kandy and Randey called Dad's mom Nana, even though they weren't related to her. "What do you think, Green?"

"I think Nana will pull up first, but that River will get in the house first." Green felt good about the logic behind their guess. River, who was more of a tidal wave, generally ran right through the door the second they were unbuckled. Meanwhile, Nana liked to check her phone before she came inside.

Green had a few minutes before breakfast, so they

took the opportunity to practice juggling. Nothing special, just a basic three-ball cascade, and reverse cascade, where you toss overhand instead of underhand. It was comforting to watch the balls float, knowing that each one was making its own figure eight in the air. They were like three infinities chasing each other in a static loop as long as Green kept up the rhythm.

"I knew it!" called Randey as Jan's blue sedan pulled up in front of the house.

"They're not here yet though!" proclaimed Kandy.

And sure enough, before Jan could unbuckle River from their car seat, Nana rolled up in her tiny orange hatchback. The two adults greeted each other and Jan gave Nana a bowl to carry into the house.

"All three of us were wrong!" Randey cried, when Nana opened the door.

"What?" Nana signed with one hand, holding the bowl filled with cantaloupe chunks in the other.

Green explained that Kandy and Randey had been guessing who would show up first.

"You were wrong too!" said Kandy, pointing at Green and repeating the sign for *wrong*.

Nana was Deaf, with fat rosy cheeks and a clever smile. She usually wore a matching set of sweatpants and T-shirt, mint green this time. Once she placed the melon on the table, she pulled Green in for a long, warm hug. Nana's hugs were the best out there, especially now that Green was almost her height and their arms were long enough to really hug her back.

Then she took out her fake teeth and turned to Kandy and Randey with an eerie grin on her face that sent them shrieking around the room in delighted fright. They were still running in circles and screaming when River opened the door and immediately joined in, even though they didn't know the cause of the chaos.

Jan had ivory skin and blond hair in a spiky hair-cut, and she wore lots of silver jewelry. She headed upstairs to fetch Lulu, and perhaps more impor-tantly, the coffee, and was back down with both in minutes. Lulu was in her plaid flannel pajamas and red fuzzy slippers, and her black wavy hair that usu-ally framed her light brown face and cascaded past her shoulders, was back in a ponytail. Jan poured them both a cup of coffee and put one into Lulu's hands.

Dad placed the pancake tray, piled high, at the cen-ter of the kitchen table. The pancakes ranged in size from tiny silver dollars to plate-sized monsters, so that you could have exactly what and as much as you wanted. As usual, Dad proclaimed that no one should wait, even though he was still at the stove.

"They call them *hotcakes* for a reason," he declared. "And don't you worry about me." With that, he put a fist-sized pancake on his own plate, ran a line of syrup across it, rolled it up, and ate it in three bites, careful not to let any syrup drip into his full beard.

Lulu and Jan helped their kids with their plates, making sure they didn't make maple syrup soup with pancake croutons, then sent them to sit at the coffee table in the living room with a warning to stay at the table until they were done and to wash their hands *with soap* and to come for a stickiness check before touching anything.

Green used to sit with the kids, but these days, they pulled a step stool up to the corner of the table and sat with the adults. They were closer in age to Kandy, Randey, and River, but there were only so many conversations about boogers you could listen to while you were trying to enjoy a delicious meal. Besides, the older Green got, the less they liked being thought of as one of the kids.

Kandy, Randey, and River were too young to know about things like having crushes on people who called themselves *cis het guys*. Not that Green wanted to talk about crushes and gender politics this morning, but it was good to know they could. Lulu and Jan were self-proclaimed nonjudgmental feminists, and Dad always said that adopting Green meant he chose them, and that included wanting to know who they really were. Even Nana was pretty cool when it came to conversations about liking people. She had mostly been single since she left her husband while Dad was a teen, but sometimes she went on a date or two and liked to brag that she dated men so handsome that the friends she played cards with got jealous.

"Pancakes, glorious pancakes!" said Lulu before taking two of the large ones.

"Thanks, Dad!" Green started with a stack of three medium-sized pancakes, and would follow up with as many silver dollars as they needed to feel too full for another bite.

"You're a treasure, Matt!" said Jan, taking a giant pancake and slathering it in butter before adding a layer of silver dollars and dousing it all in syrup. "That way, I get to eat a pancake the size of my head, but I also get a taste of crispy edge in every bite."

Nana took a giant pancake, a medium pancake, and a small pancake and called it a pancake snowman.

"You lot are so much more creative than I am, especially in the morning," said Lulu, pouring herself another cup of coffee.

Nana looked over to Green, who interpreted Lulu's comment. Nana followed a lot of the conversation on her own, since it was mostly about how delicious the pancakes were and which state made the best maple syrup, but sometimes it was good to clarify.

Once the batter had been completely transformed into golden circles of joy, Dad joined the table and stacked three large pancakes between layers of butter and Lulu's homemade strawberry jam. He claimed that nothing made him hungrier than listening to his favorite people enjoy his cooking.

And that's how the morning passed until the large pile of pancakes had become eight smaller piles, filling the stomachs of eight very happy people.

# ★ CHAPTER V ★

# DANCE LIKE RONNIE'S WATCHING

It was Thursday afternoon, and the weekly Rainbow Spectrum meeting was about to start. The room filled with the buzz of students excited about the play, on top of the regular chatter about which Miss Kris lyric was the greatest and which teachers knew the most about queer stuff, other than Mx. Abrams, of course.

Mx. Abrams asked everyone to quiet down and find a seat that wasn't someone else's lap, then called the meeting to order. "Congratulations on the effect of your action last week," she said. "I'm sure you've seen the amendment to the posters around school."

A sticker had been added to the posters for *The Wizard of Oz* auditions that read *Open Casting. Anyone is welcome to try out for any role.*

"It doesn't make the play any less old," grumbled Mika.

"I still wish we were doing *Wicked* instead," said Talia. "The music's so much better."

Mx. Abrams shrugged. "You're not necessarily wrong, either of you, but the reality is that the play is *The Wizard of Oz*. However, I'm glad Mr. Sydney did the right thing in response to your letter."

Jay raised their hand. "Actually, Tracey and I were talking about the play this weekend, and we realized something. It's cool that anyone can sign up for any part, but if someone's nonbinary, they still have to pick a character that doesn't match their gender, and that's not fair."

Green's head perked up. Green knew that. Of course they knew that. That was what they had been trying to say to Ronnie last week. But to hear it said out loud by someone else made it both more true and more upsetting.

"So it's not just that nonbinary people should get to play both boys and girls," Jay continued. "It's that all the roles are *of* boys and girls. Which is pretty much saying the rest of us never get to be a part of the story."

"Fact!" Green thumped their table with the side of their fist.

Tracey joined in. "And there's no reason the characters have to be the genders they've always been. Why are they all either boys or girls, anyway? I mean, really, who's to say scarecrows aren't enby?"

"That's a good point," said Melissa. "Why does it have to be a Tin *Man*? Why can't it be a Tin *Person*?"

"The Cowardly Lion makes sense as a guy, though," said Leila. "Girl lions are the hunters. Boy lions mostly just sit around and yawn."

"You kids don't let a beat pass, do you?" Mx. Abrams said. Then her face brightened. "And why should you? Let's see if we can get this all settled up today." She pulled out her phone and sent a text.

A few minutes later, the door opened and a tall man with carefully coiffed hair stepped in. He wore a bold purple button-down shirt and a green bow tie with purple trim.

"Mr. Sydney!" shouted most of the seventh and eighth graders as one.

"Thank you, John, for dropping by," said Mx. Abrams. "I figured you'd still be around. We've been talking about this year's school musical."

"Queer and trans youth talking theater? Why, I'd be upset if you hadn't asked me to join in. And thank you for advocating for open casting. Among other things, it'll bring a new QUILTBAG+ perspective to a story already rich in gay and lesbian history."

"That's kind of what we were talking about," said

Melissa. She explained their concern that all the parts in the play were gendered. Mr. Sydney nodded slowly as he listened. A year ago, he might have pointed out that the talking trees could be any gender you wanted, but after a year of taking criticism, he had learned that a couple of tiny roles weren't going to cut it.

Mr. Sydney had been the teacher advisor for Rainbow Spectrum last year, and while it had been a wonderful experience, it had also been challenging. These kids knew about all sorts of things he was just starting to learn about himself, and they asked important questions. He hadn't come out to anyone until he was in college, and even then, he'd spent another five years dancing with boys before he started to explore LGBTQIAP+ politics.

Mr. Sydney nodded his head and stroked his chin. "So not only open casting, but removing gender from the roles entirely."

"Or letting each actor interpret the gender of their role as they choose," amended Mx. Abrams. "I'll bet there are at least a few students who would like to play characters with genders, whether they be binary or not."

"Thank you, Mx. Abrams. You're always so conscientious when you chastise me," said Mr. Sydney. "These kids are lucky to have you."

"I'm lucky to have them!" said Mx. Abrams. "They're constantly teaching me."

"No kidding! You should have seen them schooling me the first few meetings last year. They were very kind about it. And I certainly had some catching up to do. Who knew that a cis gay white man could be behind the times?" He smiled to show it was a joke, not a blunder.

Green remembered the first meeting of Rainbow Spectrum last year, when Mr. Sydney had resisted the singular *they* at first, because it didn't sound grammatical to him. Green was still figuring out their pronouns, after trying *he* for two years and finding it wasn't really any better than *she*. It all worked out, and Mr. Sydney had even apologized the next week and thanked them for educating him, but it had been nerve-racking. So while Green liked Mr. Sydney, they also noticed when he didn't answer a question.

It seemed Ronnie noticed too. "So, what about the parts?"

"I don't see why not. Let each actor decide what gender they would like to interpret the role with."

Kelly jumped in to add, "As long as you're taking suggestions, what if we did *Wicked* instead of *The Wizard of Oz*?"

"Kelly," said Mr. Sydney, "when you can afford to pay for the rights to an award-winning contemporary Broadway musical, you let me know. I know this might not be the most *popular* choice, but I hope you will *defy* the *gravity* of your concerns and put on a show to remember."

With the unison of a show choir, the Rainbow Spectrum groaned at the *Wicked* references.

"Alright, settle down," said Mx. Abrams, while chuckling to herself. "You staying for the meeting, John?"

"Sorry, I gotta go. I'm on dinner duty all week to make up for the next two months, when I'll be getting home late after rehearsals."

Rainbow Spectrum was its usual raucousness after Mr. Sydney left, and the conversation Mx. Abrams tried to lead about coming out to siblings kept devolving into silly stories and small-group conversations.

Green was sitting next to Devon, who was the oldest of three, and who had a lot to say about how younger siblings were the worst. Dini, an Indian American kid with a slight build and thick hair who loved comics and superheroes, sat on Green's other side. He was the youngest of five, and said that older siblings were way worse.

"What about you, Green?" asked Devon.

"I'm an only child."

"Lucky," said Devon and Dini simultaneously.

Green shrugged as Devon and Dini traded stories to prove whether it was worse to be the youngest or the oldest. Green, meanwhile, was looking over at Ronnie again. They had been stealing glances his way all week, as though they would notice something that would explain the cis het thing or, perhaps, explain it away.

Eventually Mx. Abrams gave up trying to bring the group back together and announced a ten-minute dance party. She pulled out her phone and put on "We Are All Beautiful" by Miss Kris.

Leila took Melissa by the hand and pulled her up to the front of the room. Kelly was right behind them, along with Talia and Mika. They formed a circle and let loose. Tracey dragged Jay out of their chair to join them and Dini made a circle of his own near the back of the room, hands and legs flailing everywhere.

Even the kids who hadn't gotten up were at least tapping a toe or a finger, and the syncopated conga drumbeat was quickly making its way from Green's shoulders to their hips. It wasn't the kind of music Green usually listened to, but it was catchy. Miss Kris had barely reached the chorus by the time Green joined the growing circle at the front of the room.

"Dance like no one's watching!" Mika called out, throwing her hands up in the air and losing herself in the beat.

"Dance like EVERYONE'S watching!" cried Talia, before doing a full split in the middle of the circle.

The room filled with cheers and applause and

kids took turns in the center of the circle, showing off their quick feet and precise hand moves. The circle shifted, and suddenly Green was at the center. For a moment, they froze. They didn't know how to do a split, and they didn't know any cool videos from social media. But their arms took over and settled into the rehearsed groove of a juggler. They mimed throwing higher and higher, until they threw both hands into the air at once and then looked up as if the balls had drifted away. The Rainbow Spectrum cheered and Green stepped back to let Tracey take over in the center of the circle with a dazzling ballet spin.

"That was cool," said a voice behind Green, and when they turned around, they saw that Ronnie was looking directly at them. Smiling. Their heart tripped over itself.

"Thanks," they managed to say, suddenly conscious of their arms, which seemed to hang awkwardly in space now that they weren't doing their juggling move. Green tried to raise them above their head, but that was worse, and they were glad that Ronnie had turned to watch Melissa and Leila do a choreographed bit together.

The circle clapped in time around them as the two girlfriends mirrored each other's steps with giant grins on their faces, forward, back, side, side. Then they did it again, closer. And closer still, so that their sides were pressed against each other, their arms around each other's waists.

Green cheered with everyone else when the dance ended with Melissa kissing Leila on her cheek, but an unpleasant nagging sensation pointed out that no one was pressed against their side. They hoped they might accidentally bump into Ronnie, or that Ronnie would accidentally bump into them, but they kept a nervous distance that meant that the only person they bumped into was Rick in the other direction.

Rick was waving his arms around his face in a dance that was probably something from *Rogue Space* but looked more like he was swatting away mosquitoes. He wore a huge grin, and he didn't seem to care that he was the only one dancing like a space creature. He might have even liked it better that way. He didn't look nervous and he certainly didn't care who he bumped into. Green stuck to their basic shuffle and shoulder shimmy.

When Mx. Abrams announced that the third song was the last of the day, Green found themself looking for Ronnie again. He wasn't close, but he wasn't that far away either. If they didn't make a move now, it would be too late. Green took a deep breath and the tiniest of steps to the left. And again. And again. They told themself it was no big deal—they were just dancing with the group—as they made their way toward their target.

Seven thousand tiny steps later, they felt their forearm brush against something. They turned around, only to find themself facing Kelly. She took their hand in hers and twirled herself underneath the arc of their arms, then let go and danced off, leaving Green rattled and spinning a bit. By the time they reoriented and figured out where Ronnie was, the song was fading away into a flute solo that was beautiful, but not very good for dancing.

Mx. Abrams directed everyone to gather their things, and once they were ready, she escorted them out, like a herd of queer sheep.

Ronnie headed for the bus stop two blocks away, along with Rick, Jay, and a few other kids. Green walked home from school, which meant they needed to cross the street and make a right. And yet, they found themselves joining the group, walking next to Ronnie and laughing about how much fun it was to dance in the same room where they had taken vocabulary tests last year.

"I really like that juggling move you did," said Ronnie.

"Yeah, you said so." Green winced at their own words. They hadn't meant to sound rude or stupid, but they had managed to do both.

If Ronnie was offended, though, his grin didn't show it. "Yeah, well, I liked it so much I wanted to tell you twice."

"Thanks." Green could feel their face warming. "I'm glad you could tell it was supposed to be juggling."

"I wasn't sure at first, but then I remembered you juggled at last year's Cabaret Night."

"You remember that?" Green was pretty sure that counted as a compliment.

"Of course. I remember the whole show. I have a really good memory."

"Oh." Good memories weren't compliments.

"But I remember yours especially."

"That's cool." Green didn't know what else to say, but that didn't seem to matter. They wanted this moment to last as long as possible, standing next to Ronnie, their body tingling and a smile on their face that got goofier by the moment.

Green was disappointed to see the city bus in the distance, making its way down the street. When the bus arrived, Ronnie was the last to get on. Green watched him through the windows, walking down the aisle and already laughing at something Rick had said. Green couldn't help wishing they had been the one to say something that made Ronnie laugh.

# ★ CHAPTER VI ★

# AUDITIONS

Over the next few days, Green found themself wondering what it would be like to play a nonbinary scarecrow. To be onstage without it mattering whether they were acting like a boy or a girl, the same as when they had juggled in last year's Cabaret Night. Having everyone stare at you because you were doing something cool was way better than when they stared because they were trying to figure out what you were.

An image kept popping into Green's mind at odd moments—during an ad before an online video, while they were brushing their teeth, in between math questions in class—of how they would look in overalls and a straw hat, as if they already had the part. In front of the mirror at home, they practiced making their body look all wobbly, as if they were stuffed with straw instead of bones. And when they supposedly got a brain from the Wizard, they could show off by juggling.

Tuesday was the slowest day in the history of Jung Middle School. At least, that's the way it felt to Green.

At lunch, the unofficial Rainbow Spectrum table was filled with chatter about who wanted which parts and who should get them. Even kids who didn't usually eat with Green and the bunch joined in the gossip.

Dini wanted to be the Wizard himself. "I am the great and powerful Oz!" he proclaimed.

"The Wizard is a fraud!" said Leila. "That's why I'm trying out for Glinda, the Good Witch of the North."

"So is Tracey!" said Kelly.

"I wouldn't want to have to make that decision," said Rick.

"My mom wants me to try out for Toto." Talia made an unpleasant face. "But I want to be the Wicked Witch."

"You'd make a *great* villain!" Mika high-fived Talia. "I don't even know what part I want. I'm gonna read the Lion's part, because it's a funny scene, but I'm gonna tell Mr. Sydney I could play any role."

"Not Dorothy, you can't!" said Kelly. Everyone was sure that Melissa should be Dorothy, and Melissa didn't disagree. She just smiled shyly and said something about feeling more comfortable onstage than off.

"So, are you going to try out?" Green asked Ronnie, thinking maybe they could practice their lines together while they waited.

"Nah," said Ronnie. "I'm purely a backstage kinda

guy. I'm gonna be in the crew!" He pointed his thumb at his chest and smiled proudly.

"Oh." Green hoped they didn't sound too disappointed. They would still get to hang out backstage a bit. And at least Ronnie didn't want to be the Scarecrow too. That would have been dreadful.

No one asked Green what part they were going to try out for, and while they sort of wished that someone—maybe Ronnie—would ask, they were also sort of glad not to have to answer the question. Saying it out loud would make the audition a little realer, especially the part where they might not get the role.

And it wasn't just their group who was excited. When Kelly and Leila busted out a chorus of "Over the Rainbow," kids from at least three other tables sang along too. No matter how old-fashioned and uncool the choice of musical was, the chance to be a star was still alluring.

After school, the buzz of students waiting to add their names to the sign-in sheet could be heard and felt outside the auditorium. Mx. Abrams handed out practice parts and encouraged kids to wait inside once they had signed up, instead of forming a mass in the hallway.

Green signed in and joined a cluster of Rainbow Spectrum kids in the front row of seats, rehearsing their lines to themselves and each other. Green took the seat all the way on the end of the row, where they could see into the backstage wing on the other side.

Mr. Sydney and Ms. Jones had already gotten started in a small room behind the stage. Green could see Mr. Sydney through the door window, in his navy shirt and red bow tie, but in the busy auditorium, you couldn't hear each kid singing over the muffled piano. Green was glad for that. Even though the eventual plan involved singing in front of a full audience, somehow the idea that people could be listening in was pretty embarrassing. Green was trying out in spite of the singing, not because of it.

Green was also glad that the singing part of the auditions didn't last very long. From the sounds of the piano, most kids sang only one verse. Green wondered whether that was a good sign or a bad one. Maybe the teachers were so impressed they didn't need to hear more. Or maybe they wanted to give their ears a break.

One by one, Mx. Abrams called for kids to join Mr. Sydney and Ms. Jones. Eventually Melissa was called. Then Leila. Then Green. They exchanged a pair of thumbs-ups with Mx. Abrams on their way in.

Mr. Sydney sat at the piano, while Ms. Jones was at a student desk with a spread of papers filled with notes. The room was even smaller than Green had expected, and they pressed their back against the door.

"Part?" Ms. Jones asked curtly.

"Th-the Scarecrow," Green whispered, hoping that didn't count as part of the audition.

"No need to worry," said Mr. Sydney. "Just show us what you've got." He tickled a little trill out of the piano keys. "You ready?"

"Um, yeah," Green said, and the intro to "If I Only Had a Brain" started. Their mind went blank and they had to look at the sheet to remember the first words of the song. That put them a moment behind the beat. Ms. Jones frowned. Green tried to catch up but ended up singing the second line too fast. Ms. Jones wrote a note on one of the papers in front of her. Green closed their eyes, trying not to think about what she was writing, and was glad when they got to the "if I only had a brain" part of the song and Mr. Sydney stopped playing.

Then it was time to read the dialogue, with Ms. Jones reading the other parts. Green's brain cycled through a dozen thoughts about whether their singing had been terrible, or just mediocre, and how much it mattered that they had flubbed the beginning. By the time they really got into the scene, there were only two lines left to read. They read them with as much gusto as they could and hoped for the best.

"Thanks for your time, Green," said Mr. Sydney politely, without a hint of emotion that might have signaled how he felt about their performance.

They stepped out of the small room and Mx. Abrams called the next kid in to audition. Green wished luck to Mika, who hadn't auditioned yet, and Talia, who had, but was waiting around for Mika.

On the walk home, Green's worries about the audition itself faded back into the excitement of playing the Scarecrow. No one had sung for very long in their audition, and they didn't know anyone else trying for that part. Probably everyone had made some kind of mistake in their audition, except maybe Melissa.

Green pictured themself with straw coming out of their flannel shirt and overalls, pointing in opposite directions with crossed arms as they announced, "Of course, some people do go *both* ways!"

It was hands down Green's favorite line in the movie version, when Dorothy asked the Scarecrow about which way to get to the Wizard, and they were sure they could play it up. Maybe they'd even change the line to "some people go *lots* of ways!" and point all over the place.

Green was still smiling about the idea when they reached a small park a few blocks from school. As on most afternoons, a line of six women in pastel athletic wear jogged in a circle around the block.

They would loop around the tree-lined sidewalk a few times before congratulating one another over bottles of water and heading to their cars.

The usual group of boys from school sat on the large play structure of turrets, slides, bridges, and platforms that filled one corner of the park, and when the women lapped around, they would cheer and clap. Green couldn't tell whether the applause was supposed to be sarcastic, but the women cheered back.

The boys generally left Green alone, but to be safe, Green kept their eyes on the far side of the street as they passed the playground. They could hear the boys talking as they approached.

"Did you hear?" said a voice that could only be Jeff's. Jeff was a complete jerk of a kid. He even talked like a bully would, with a voice that he made deeper than it naturally was.

Jeff went on. "They're going to let anyone try

out for any part in the play. Boys playing girls. Girls playing boys. Whatever-they-ares playing whatever-they-ares."

"So?" asked one of the other boys. "You got something against that?"

"I just think it's too much," Jeff said. He sounded like the kind of parent who Green's dad said was afraid of learning new things. Probably his own parent.

"What do you care anyway?" a third boy asked. "Are you planning to be in the play?"

Jeff hit him on the shoulder. "No."

"You sure? You seem to know a lot about it."

"No," said Jeff, "I mean, yes. I mean, I'm sure I'm not gonna be in some dumb play. Plays are for babies."

"Perfect for you, you mean?"

"Shut up, Jarrett."

"What, is the baby sleepy? Does the baby need a naptime?"

"SHUT UP!"

Green smiled but kept from laughing out loud until he was at least a block away. There was no reason to tempt fate, especially when a crowd of junior high school boys was involved. Still, it was nice to see them take down one of their own a bit.

## ★ CHAPTER VII ★

# IF I ONLY HAD
# A PART

Mr. Sydney had promised the cast list would be posted online by 4 p.m. Thursday, and throughout the day, students were sneaking out their phones in case he finished early. By the start of Rainbow Spectrum, most of the group had their phones in their hands. It was after-school hours, so technically they were allowed to have them out, but most kids kept them in their bags or pockets during Rainbow Spectrum meetings unless there was something to research. It was 3:10 p.m. though, and the cast list would be up in less than an hour. That definitely qualified as something to research every few seconds, to see if there had been an update.

Green noticed that Ronnie was one of the few kids not checking his phone. Even Kelly, who was going to be in the band, was refreshing the page to make sure that Melissa would be cast as Dorothy. Ronnie was lucky: He didn't have to audition to be a stagehand and then wait twenty-four hours to find out whether he had been the best at wearing black and making sure the props were in the right places. Green refreshed the site again, hoping to see *Scarecrow: Green Gibson,* but the page just thanked everyone for trying out and hoped that anyone who didn't receive a speaking role would consider joining the ensemble cast, band, or crew.

"I see where your brains are," said Mx. Abrams, after a third person didn't realize it was their turn to check in because they were reloading the site. "How about we designate one person at a time on Cast List Watch while the rest of us focus on the meeting?"

Once they had set a schedule of ten-minute shifts, the group got back to check-in and then the main topic for the day.

"Unless anyone has other pressing issues?" Mx. Abrams asked, as she did every week. Sometimes, someone had a problem at home they wanted to talk about, or maybe they wanted to share news about books being challenged at a school library somewhere. Today, the room was quiet. Shaking with energy, but quiet.

"In that case, I thought we might talk about LGBTQIAP+ connections to theater," said Mx. Abrams. "Performance is very queer, you know."

"Mx. Abrams," called out Tracey, "are you stereotyping all theater people as gay?"

"No," said Mx. Abrams, "but thank you for asking. I'm not saying that *everyone* in theater is part of the queer community, or that every queer and trans person is interested in theater. But there is a set of rich and complex connections between the two communities. The same stage that allows us to put on a mask sometimes allows us to reveal our truest selves."

"Deep," said Kelly.

"In fact," added Mx. Abrams, "gender theorists like Judith Butler explore the idea that all gender is performative. It's not who you are, but what you do, one of the ways you present yourself to the world. In other words, how you *perform* in the play we call life."

"For sure," said Em, a small but rugged sixth grader in jeans and a plaid flannel shirt. "Every day, when I get dressed, it's like I'm saying who I'm gonna be that day."

"Totally!" Green nodded emphatically.

"I kinda walk different when I'm wearing a sparkly outfit for dance," said Devon. "Even when I'm not onstage. I definitely feel more genderfluid when I wear sparkles."

"Wait," said Dini. "Are you saying sparkles are gendered?"

"Great question!" said Mx. Abrams, trying to gather the five small conversations about the gender of sparkles that erupted around the room. "*Are sparkles gendered?*"

"They can be," said Melissa. "But I don't think they have to be. I mean, I'm a girl, and I wear a lot of sparkles, yeah, but I don't wear sparkles because I'm a girl, and I'm not a girl because I wear sparkles. Take my older brother, Scott. He's as straight-boy as they come. But sometimes he wears nail polish. He says it's beautiful, plus it hides his dirty fingernails from football practice."

The room filled with so many follow-up points that Mx. Abrams had to call on people by hand. Most kids wanted to talk about sparkles, but Green was more interested in the idea that gender was a performance. Sometimes Green felt like they were acting, especially when they decided not to wear a pink clip or a glittery pair of sunglasses because they didn't want people to assume that they were a girl. Which, Green realized, came right back to the question of whether sparkles were gendered or whether it was all an act. Maybe they would wear something sparkly to be a nonbinary scarecrow. That is, if they got the part.

The meeting went well, even if the group was a bit jumpy. "Is it up?" was called out more than once after someone coughed.

It wasn't until the second-to-last shift of Cast List Watch that Kelly screamed, "Melissa! You're Dorothy!"

Even Leila, who had been in the middle of talking about Marlene Dietrich, a bisexual woman actor from black-and-white films who used to dress in tuxedos and top hats, finished abruptly with, "And so, like, that was cool," then pulled out her phone.

Within moments, everyone in the room had either read the list on their phone or someone else's, and the room was filled with congratulations, especially for Melissa.

"I knew it!" said Kelly. "Melissa shines onstage."

"Uh, we know!" said Tracey. "Why do you think we made her emcee of last year's Cabaret Night? As a sixth grader, no less! Yeah, this is Melissa's world, and we're all just living in it." She turned to Melissa. "No shade. You're fabulous."

"Why thank you," Melissa said with a softness that both acknowledged the compliment and her slight discomfort with it. "And congratulations to you too!" Tracey's name had been listed next to the Wicked Witch of the West.

Green scrolled down the list, and then back up. They did it again, and a third time, in case they had missed something. They stared at the screen. Some kid whose name Green didn't recognize would be playing the Scarecrow. Green's name wasn't on the list at all. Not even as the Munchkin mayor or something.

The room was noisy, but from a distance. They felt warm. Or the air felt warm, it was hard to tell. Their body seemed to have turned inside out.

The room was still a chaos of bodies hugging and dancing around when the door opened and Mr. Sydney poked his head in. That day's bow tie was cobalt blue with silver threads, and his collared shirt was white.

"Hey, kids. Hey, Mx. Abrams. I hope you don't mind the interruption."

Mx. Abrams laughed. "Mr. Sydney, you interrupted the moment you decided to post the cast list during Rainbow Spectrum."

"Fair point," said Mr. Sydney. "Anyway, I figured that a few of my cast members would be here, so I'm excited to congratulate Melissa, who will be our

Dorothy, as well as Tracey, Dini, Leila, Em, Mika, and Talia." His eyes swept across the room, comparing who was there with the cast list in his hand. "I'll get each of you scripts tomorrow so you can start learning your lines. If you play an instrument, Ms. Han will be speaking with you about whether you'd like to be in our pit band. And I'd like to remind the rest of you that you are encouraged to join the crew, who will perform all the needed magic to pave the Yellow Brick Road."

After Mr. Sydney left, it was nearly 4 p.m. and the end of Rainbow Spectrum for the week.

"Alright, my queer little chickadees," said Mx. Abrams, then added before Kelly could finish raising her hand, "and the rest of you too. I love you all, but I gotta get home to Tim and Max, so let's make with the gathering of things and promenade to the front door so I can say I saw you safely leave the building."

Green held their bag and jacket in their hand, but they didn't want to get up until the very last moment. They weren't sure they *could* get up.

"Hey," said a voice behind them. A very cute voice.

"Hey."

"What's the matter?" asked Ronnie. "Didn't get the part you wanted?"

"Didn't get a part at all."

"That sucks."

"Yeah, it does. It's funny, I wasn't even interested in being in a play until last week, and now it feels awful."

"Emotions are weird."

"I hate group projects. Why would I want to do one after school? But I was excited about it."

"You could always be in the ensemble," Ronnie offered.

"It's not the same," Green mumbled noncommittally.

"Or maybe the crew. I'll be on the crew."

"I'll think about it," said Green with a bit of smile. Another image flashed by in their mind, this time of Ronnie and Green carrying furniture onstage together.

"C'mon," said Mx. Abrams impatiently from the doorway. "Time to go."

Green looked around. Only they and Ronnie were still in the classroom. They stood with a screech of their chair and walked alongside Ronnie. They trailed behind the group of kids on their way to the bus stop. Neither of them said much, but it was nice to be together.

"Which way do you live, by the way?" asked Ronnie, once they reached the crowded stop.

Green pointed back in the direction of their house.

"Then why did you come this way?" asked Ronnie.

Green couldn't think of any answer but the truth. "I was enjoying walking with you."

"Well, I enjoyed walking with you too." Ronnie grinned.

After that, Green didn't know quite what to say, and was glad it was Ronnie's turn to get on the bus. But they still waited until the bus left before crossing the street. When the traffic light changed and the bus drove by, Green waved, and Ronnie waved back.

# ★ CHAPTER VIII ★

# SHIPWRECK

That evening, Dad was trimming his beard, with his leather case of tools unzipped and spread out on the counter next to the bathroom sink. The air smelled of mint and soap. Searching his face in the mirror carefully, he clipped out-of-place hairs. His was an impressively full beard, longer than the width of his hand when he stroked it, which was often.

Green stood in the mirror next to him and explored their face. It was rosy peach and round, with cheeks that got even rounder when Green smiled. Their hair was mostly cut close to their head, except for the green wave that fell just over one eye, that they had been growing since the end of fifth grade, when they convinced Dad to shave the rest. Lulu had helped them start dying it Atomic Alligator green that summer.

Green thought it might be cool to have a beard themself someday, but that would mean taking testosterone, a hormone that would have all sorts of other effects on their mind and body, including possibly growing less hair on the top of their head when they got older. Green wasn't ready to make that decision, at least not yet, which didn't matter because they couldn't get a prescription at their age.

Their doctor had mentioned hormone blockers, which weren't hormones themselves, but would stop estrogen and other chemicals already in their body from running all the puberty programs. The doctor said that they were the right age for treatment if they chose it, and she was probably right, since their body was starting to get a little curvier, both at their chest and around their hips. But when Green looked in the mirror, they liked the way their body flowed. They sometimes thought about having a curvy body and a beard at the same time, and that sounded like they would need more hormones, not fewer.

Green didn't say all of this to Dad though. As close as they were, it wasn't exactly parent talk, at least not for Green. Still, they did want to ask about something else.

"Um, Dad?"

"What's up?" Dad kept his eyes on the mirror, hunting for straggler curls.

"The ceiling." It had been their joke for so long that it wasn't really funny anymore, but it also didn't feel right not to say it.

"Anything else?"

"Well, yeah, actually. Let's say there's this kid. And let's say this kid is straight."

Dad put down the scissors and looked over at Green. "Real kid or hypothetical kid?"

"Hypothetical," said Green. True, Ronnie was real, but it didn't have to be about just Ronnie. It could be anyone.

"Does it matter, boy or girl?"

"Does it ever?"

Dad shrugged. "You're the one who made them straight." Green slumped to the ground. For half a moment, they wished they could have a normal parent. Then they remembered Melissa talking about having to convince her mom that she was a girl, and Jay, whose parents still used their old name at home. Normal had its problems.

"Boy," said Green.

"Okay." Dad sat on the edge of the tub.

"Now let's say that kid likes a bisexual girl. That doesn't matter, right?"

"Of course not."

"Or a transgender girl," said Green.

"Girls are girls, so I don't see why you're even

asking." Dad was a proud trans-inclusive femi-nist. He even had a shirt that said so, which Green thought was cool most of the time, except when Dad pointed it out, which was extremely uncool.

"Well, what if this straight boy likes someone nonbinary?"

"Hunh," said Dad, "That's a good question. What do you think?"

Classic parental redirect. Luckily, Green had been dealing with Dad all their life and was ready.

"I think I'd like to know what you think."

"Clever," said Dad. "I think that how two people get along and treat each other is what's important."

"Okay, but that means they aren't straight any-more, doesn't it?"

"I'm saying that people get to define their own relationships."

"I know that!" said Green.

"Do you?" said Dad.

Of course they did. Didn't they?

"It's also good to check in with other people in your boat though," said Dad, getting up to put away his beard-trimming kit.

"What boat?"

"Well, I'm on the U.S.S. *Cis Het White Guy.*"

"Dad, that's not one boat. That's a fleet."

Dad laughed. "Fair enough. I'm on the one for Sensitive Rockers. Point is, I'm your dad, and I love you, and I'm always here for you, but also, I'm not a nonbinary kid growing up in the twenty-first century. Couldn't hurt to talk with someone a little more like you about this."

Dad had a point.


The next day, Green saw Ronnie heading toward the bus stop. They thought about joining him, but they felt silly now that Ronnie knew they didn't live in that direction. Besides, Ronnie and Rick were so thick in conversation they might not have known anyone else was around.

Green wished they had a best friend like that. Or like Mika and Talia, who became super close once they stopped trying to date each other and getting in fights over it. Even Dad and Lulu had each other. Some people had two people, like Melissa, who had a best friend and a girlfriend. Green had lots of friends, or at least, people they were friendly with. But they didn't have that one special person.

They saw Jay walking half a block ahead of them. Their sandy blond hair was cut short all-round, leaving a pile of semicircles on their head. They wore a blue plaid shirt and blue jeans, with black sneakers and a plain black backpack.

Green's bag wasn't as busy as Rick's, who covered his with as many buttons and pins as would fit, but they had a few queer patches and a glittery button that said *I Believe in Unicorns*. And their hair matched their name, of course.

Not that you had to look cool to be cool, or even that cool was an important thing to be, but your style was a way to say who you were, and Jay seemed to be saying they were someone to look past. Even their name was pretty nondescript. If you were going to take a letter for your name, you could be Vee or Ess or any letter you wanted. Maybe even Zed, which was how you said Zee in Canada. Zed was a cool name. Not that you needed a cool name to be cool. There were probably lots of exciting, outgoing people named Jay, but this Jay wasn't one of them.

Still, though, they were the only other nonbinary kid Green knew of at school, or at least the only one who used *they* pronouns exclusively. Em was enby, and used *they* at Rainbow Spectrum, but they used *she* and *her* in class and at home. There were also a few kids at Rainbow Spectrum who introduced themselves with "she or they, it doesn't really matter," but most of them startled when Green actually used the second option. For the other kids, *they* was always the second option.

Green may not have wanted it to matter, but it mattered. Everyone had the right to what worked for them, but Jay was the only other kid who knew about having to decide when and how to correct your teachers when they used the wrong pronouns for you.

Jay had started going to Rainbow Spectrum at the beginning of last year, same as Green. They started using *they/them* pronouns soon after and changed their name to Jay. At the end of the year, they started dating Tracey, who was pretty cool, so they must have had something going for them.

Green walked a little more quickly to catch up. "Whatcha doing tomorrow?" they said to Jay.

"Not much. Why?"

"You want to hang out?"

"Maybe?" They sounded uncertain.

Green backpedaled. "You don't have to if you don't want to."

"Nah, it's cool. I have to check with my mom first. But I don't think we're doing anything."

Green sighed with relief. "And I mean, it's not like I'm asking you on a date or anything. I just thought we could watch some TV or talk or whatever."

"Good, because Tracey and I are exclusive."

"Cool."

"Cool."

And that's how Green ended up on the porch at home on Saturday afternoon, juggling and waiting for Jay to arrive. Lulu, Jan, and the kids had stayed after pancake brunch to watch a movie, and everyone but Green had fallen asleep before the teenage superhero even discovered her powers, so Green had turned off the television and come out to the front porch.

They were practicing juggling four balls at once, which meant that they had to manage two in their left hand and two in their right. They were pretty good with their right hand, and so-so with their left, but when they tried both hands at once, it was less like juggling and more like throwing the balls in the air and watching them hit the ground. If they could ever get the hang of it, they could show everyone at Rainbow Spectrum. No one else there juggled, not even Dini, who did magic tricks, but that was one of the best things about Rainbow Spectrum—there, unusual was a good thing.

Green lived on a big enough road that there was generally a moving car in sight, whether approaching or already gone by, and Green played a game of guessing which car was likely to be Jay's. Not the purple minivan, not the black Jeep, definitely not the white delivery truck. Maybe the small blue car with the wide highlights. Maybe the third of three white sedans in a row. It looked like it was driving slowly to read house numbers. Eventually a *definite maybe* of a silver hatchback pulled to a stop and Jay popped out of the back seat.

"Hey!" said Green.

"Hey!" said Jay. "Why are you outside?"

"What's wrong with outside?" They dropped the juggling balls into a bucket.

"Nothing, I guess. It's just that I thought we were going to watch TV."

Green explained that their dad, Lulu, and the twins were probably still asleep, and that if they woke Kandy and Randey, they would have to either watch them or make Dad or Lulu get up, neither of which was a very good idea.

"Don't you have a TV in your room?"

"The TV's in the family room. Dad and I usually watch stuff together." Once they said it, they felt a weird pang of shame. Weird because they had never really cared about not having a television in their room. They knew a lot of kids at school did, but they didn't mind sharing with Dad. "We could watch something on my tablet."

"Tablet screens are tiny."

"Okay." Green felt awkward. "Let's just hang out here, then."

Jay took the seat next to Green and pulled out their phone. "We could listen to some music."

For a flash, Green wondered what it would feel like to listen to music on a phone with Ronnie, then shook the idea from their mind. Ronnie wasn't there.

"Do you ever listen to Metallica?" Green asked.

"That old heavy metal band?"

"They're not that old." Green knew it was wrong

the moment they said it. "Or, well, even if they are, their music's pretty cool. Their early stuff anyway."

"Hipster much?" said Jay.

"What?"

"*Their first album was better* is like a total hipster slogan."

Green wasn't entirely sure what a hipster was, only that it didn't sound like a good thing to be. Jay played some electronic pop song about getting up to get down to dance even though they just sat there.

If Green was going to have a new friend, they were going to be the kind of person who would get up to get down and look just as silly as Green as they made themselves laugh until they thought they might pass out from lack of oxygen.

Green and Jay may have been on the same ship, but they were definitely on different decks. They didn't laugh once, not even after Kandy and Randey woke up and they went inside to watch videos. Jay kept wanting to watch clips where people did stupid things and got hurt, and he called Green's favorite video of all time, the adorable one about a small turtle taking a ride on a larger turtle, "probably fake or something."

Ronnie wouldn't call it fake, even if he thought it was. Well, him, or most people. Green certainly wasn't thinking especially about Ronnie. Melissa wouldn't have called it fake, or Rick either. Okay, fine, Kelly might have, but she would be interested in figuring out how they did it. And none of them would have implied that there was anything wrong with thinking it was a cool video. Jay may have looked like a perfect friend on paper, but reality wasn't much of a reader.

# ★ CHAPTER IX ★

# WHEN PIGS FLY

Green was disappointed not to be the Scarecrow in the play, but the more time passed, the more they were also relieved not to have to sing onstage. Not to mention how itchy the costume must be, with all that hay stuffed everywhere, and having to memorize pages worth of lines.

Still, there was something electric about being part of a group of people preparing for a big show. Rainbow Spectrum's Cabaret Night last year had been epic, and not just because people applauded when Green juggled onstage. It was like you were suddenly part of a new, extended family. There were special cues you all learned and in-jokes that no one else understood.

That's when they remembered there was another way to be part of the show, one that didn't require an audition. Yeah, it would have been fun to play a nonbinary scarecrow and hang out with kids like Melissa, but there was someone Green was even more eager to spend more time with.

Green spotted him the moment he got to the schoolyard, the sun highlighting the red undertones of his brown curls. He was hanging out with Melissa, Kelly, Leila, and Rick, a queer island among a sea of middle schoolers waiting for the front doors to open.

"Guess what?" said Green, giving an extra-wide smile to Ronnie. Ronnie smiled back, and Green felt ticklish on the inside.

"Aliens are real," said Melissa.

"And you're one of them!" added Kelly. The best

friends turned to each other and screamed with wide-open mouths until they both broke into peals of laughter.

Leila shook her head.

"Don't yuck their yum," Rick said to Leila, "just because they have a connection that isn't based on romance."

"I'm not yucking their yum because they're best friends. I'm just saying they're ridiculous."

"Nothing wrong with being ridiculous," Rick pointed out.

"So," said Ronnie, turning from Leila to Green. "What's the news?"

The tickle in Green's stomach grew. Saying it made it real. "I'm joining the stage crew!"

"Yes!" said Ronnie, with a fist pump that turned Green's insides into a full-blown tornado. Ronnie might not mark all the checkboxes for a nonbinary kid's friend-who-was-cute-and-maybe-something-else-might-happen, but the idea of spending more time with him sure did sound like fun.

And it was. The first meeting for Jung Middle School's production of *The Wizard of Oz* included everyone—cast, crew, and band. There were so many people from Rainbow Spectrum there, it almost felt like a meeting. But instead of talking about whatever they felt like, Mr. Sydney announced that they had a strict schedule and no time to waste. Of course, that didn't stop him from opening with a long speech about the wonders of theater and the history of *The Wizard of Oz* as an important institution, both for the school and for musical productions everywhere.

"And that, my young performers and creators," said Mr. Sydney, "brings us to today. I'd like to thank both Ms. Jones, who will be supporting the crew, and Ms. Han, who will lead the band.

"The cast and band will be rehearsing separately,

at least for now, so we won't all be together like this every day. But while I have you here, I'd like to share a concern that was raised to me recently. *The Wizard of Oz* is an old musical, based on an even older book. And sometimes, we'll need to make changes in order to create a production we can be proud of. So I'd like your help in thinking something through."

Green wondered whether Mr. Sydney was talking about the genders of roles, but that had already been decided.

As if he'd heard what Green was thinking, Mr. Sydney continued, "You all know that everyone is encouraged to play their roles as the gender of their choice, and we will make adjustments to the script as necessary. For example, I believe we will be having a Tin Queer this year."

A tall kid Green didn't know saluted in response. "Yes, please!"

"But there's another issue with the script that

needs to be addressed. Does one of the people who brought the issue to my attention want to say more?"

"I can, if no one else wants to," said Dini. He looked around, but no one raised a hand, and a couple of kids nodded for him to continue. "Okay, so the flying monkeys. Some of us were talking, and it's not that monkeys are racist, but sometimes Black people have been compared to monkeys, which *is* pretty racist. So it's kinda sketchy to have them be the servants for the Wicked Witch."

The room filled with nods, *ohhhs*, and *yeahs*, and a couple of kids whistled in support.

"Preach!" Tracey exclaimed.

"It is an excellent point," said Mr. Sydney. "And wonderfully put. Thanks, Dini, and everyone who was part of that conversation. So, are we in agreement that the flying monkeys are a problem? Show of hands?"

Green raised their hand immediately, and when they looked around, they couldn't see a hand that wasn't up. Kelly had two hands up. Green had never thought about the flying monkeys being a problem, but now that Dini mentioned it, they were really glad Mr. Sydney wanted to change it.

"Any suggestions of what to do instead?" asked Mr. Sydney. "Maybe some other animal? One that doesn't traditionally have wings?"

"Pigs!" Kelly cried.

"Pigs?" Tracey looked like she didn't like pigs very much.

"Why pigs?" asked Ronnie.

"Haven't you heard the saying that something will happen when pigs fly?" asked Kelly.

"But doesn't that mean something that never happens?" asked Leila.

"Well, have you ever seen *The Wizard of Oz* with flying pigs before?" Kelly pointed out.

"I think it's funny," said Mika.

"Me too," said Talia.

"Aren't pig costumes going to cost money?" asked the girl who was playing the Tin Queer.

"Sure," said Mr. Sydney. "But this is important."

"And I'm sure the crew and I will be able to come up with something without too much strain on the budget," said Ms. Jones.

"Wonderful!" Mr. Sydney exclaimed. "Before we decide, is anyone unhappy with pigs?"

Nearly fifty kids looked at Dini.

"Don't look at me! I love it!" Dini exclaimed.

"Are there any other suggestions that we should consider?" asked Mr. Sydney.

Nearly fifty kids shook their heads.

"In that case, flying pigs it is!"

"Nicely done!" said Ms. Jones. "I can tell this is going to be a great group to work with."

"I'm glad we were able to solve that so quickly," said Mr. Sydney. "As we move forward, if you notice something else about your part or the play that's not working for you, I hope you'll feel comfortable raising the issue. For now, let's get into groups and start working."

Mr. Sydney brought the cast onstage while Ms. Han met with the band in the back of the auditorium. Only six kids were there for the crew, so Ms. Jones took them out into the hall, where it was quieter, and gathered them into a circle to talk about what a crew does and what each kid might like to work on.

Ronnie was on Green's left. Green moved a little closer, and then a little more, until they could feel that their T-shirt was touching Ronnie's. They held their breath as tightly as their body, and they could feel the heat of Ronnie's shoulder on theirs. They relaxed slowly until their upper arm rested lightly against Ronnie's. They breathed softly, not wanting to startle Ronnie and lose contact, but on the inside, their body had turned into a container of high-bounce balls ricocheting about.

By the time it was their turn to say what they wanted to work on, all they came up with was, "I like paint," like a toddler who was just learning how language worked. Ms. Jones nodded politely.

Ronnie went next. "I like paint too!" he said proudly, with a quick grin in Green's direction. "Really, though, I love everything behind the scenes. I especially love pulling up the stage curtain on the night of the show. I did it for the Rainbow Spectrum's Cabaret Night last year and it's really cool to be the one who actually starts the performance! If no one raises the curtain, it doesn't matter what any of the actors do."

"Your enthusiasm is most welcome, Ronnie," said Ms. Jones before moving on to the next kid.

When everyone had spoken, Ms. Jones thanked them for sharing. "You are an engaged bunch! In fact, we might be able to work on a special project this year, yes?" The group met her question with a cheer. "I was thinking maybe we could build a few new set pieces. I know the woodworking teacher over at the high school, and she said she has some students who might want to come help us out. What do you think?"

"Awesome!" said Ronnie.

Everyone else agreed, including Green, even though they were a little intimidated by the idea of hammers and saws. If Ronnie thought it was a good idea, it probably was.

Green could still feel the echo of Ronnie's arm against theirs as they walked home. But maybe the shoulder press had been nothing. It had to have meant nothing. Maybe Ronnie's shirt was thicker and he hadn't even realized their shoulders were touching.

Ronnie had called himself a heterosexual guy, and no matter what Dad said about people defining their own relationships, Green was pretty sure that meant Ronnie liked girls. Maybe Ronnie was just being nice when he had acted like *I like paint* wasn't a stupid thing to say. There was no way Green was a girl, and they were pretty sure Ronnie knew that. At least they hoped Ronnie knew that.

Or maybe it did mean something. After all, some pigs *did* fly.

# ★ CHAPTER X ★

# NO LIMITS

The week couldn't pass quickly enough for Green. Not even Rainbow Spectrum was as exciting as the idea of getting back to working on the play. Apparently, there was a lot more to crew than liking paint. Green and Ronnie had been talking whenever they got a chance about how much fun it was all going to be. Mostly Ronnie talked, since he had been on crew last year, but Green was happy to listen. Green liked that Ronnie was so excited about something they were going to do together, and it was always nice to see him smile.

By the time Ms. Jones explained at the following Tuesday's rehearsal that the crew would be divided into three teams, Green already knew from Ronnie that the groups would be stagehands, lighting, and run-of-show. They also knew that Ronnie wanted to be on run-of-show, because those were the people who handled the curtains. Green wanted to be on run-of-show too.

"Of course, these are your *performance* roles," Ms. Jones said. "When everything needs to happen at once. Until the day of the show, we are a single team, and we will work on our projects together. Today's project"—she paused for effect—"is *wardrobe recon!*"

Seven students looked at her blankly.

"*Livery inventory!*" Ms. Jones announced.

"Liver what?" Kadyn, a short and quick eighth grader who wore a black T-shirt that said *Go Local Sportsball Team!*, wrinkled her nose.

"Costume count?" Ms. Jones offered.

"You want us to count how many costumes we need?" asked Brinley, a sixth grader with curly, light brown hair and about fifty thin plastic necklaces of varying lengths and colors.

"I want us to check on how many costumes we have, and in what sizes. Plus the props and scenery. To the theater storeroom!"

The group followed Ms. Jones behind the stage to a space somewhere between a large closet and a small room. Costumes packed a long rack, with a flock of feather boas hanging off the side. A few were protected in garment bags, but most hung loose. A silver sleeve stuck out here, a red belt there. Behind it, the walls were lined with deep shelves that ran six feet up, crammed with props from a dozen different shows. A single bare bulb hung from the ceiling.

Ms. Jones rolled out the wardrobe rack and tasked Brinley and Violet with finding the Oz costumes and giving them to cast members to try on.

"Each costume should have a tag with the name of the show and a number on it," said Ms. Jones.

"Make a list of which number costume you give to which actor."

Green looked at the rows and rows of props, boxes, and other accessories that lined the shelves of the storeroom. There was one whole section labeled *Oz*, but Green saw the Tin Queer's oil can along with a bunch of cowboy hats, and wondered what else might be on a mystery shelf. Ms. Jones gave Kadyn, Victor, and Cindy a long list and pointed to a table backstage where they should lay out everything they found.

"What are we going to do?" Ronnie sounded excited for a task, and Green was excited that Ronnie had included them in the question.

"I was hoping the two of you could help with the backdrops." Ms. Jones smiled.

"Yes!" Ronnie pumped his fist.

Green knew that Ronnie thought that the heavy

canvas scenery backdrops were almost as cool as the theater curtains themselves.

Ms. Jones led them to a corner of the backstage, where more than a dozen rolls of canvas ten feet long rested in a pile against the wall.

"They're heavy, so be careful," she warned. "Roll them, don't lift them. But two of them should say *Oz Act One* and *Oz Act Two*. Pull them out and roll them over there." She pointed to the rear of the stage, where the two backdrops would be hooked up to pulleys.

Ms. Jones was right, the backdrops were heavy, but with two people rolling them, they were more awkward than anything else. It worked better when Green and Ronnie counted together as they rolled, but more often than not, they just laughed and let the heavy tubes of canvas knock into each other.

By the time rehearsal was nearly over, they had

rolled the right two backdrops over to the pulleys and gotten the rest back into a pile. The prop table was full and the actors had each been assigned a costume.

"See, I told you crew would be fun!" Ronnie said to Green.

"It might even be more fun than Rainbow Spectrum!" Green replied.

"Wow!" Ronnie's surprise was genuine. "I know how much you love Rainbow Spectrum."

"I do," said Green. "It's cool that you come too!"

"Of course I do! It's the best!"

"I mean..." Green felt themself fumbling for words and stopped short.

"You mean?" Ronnie beamed from his pink sneakers to the little curl of brown hair that fell over his forehead.

"I mean, I think it's cool that you're part of the community even if you're, you know, straight."

"About that . . ." He trailed off.

Green perked up. "Yes?"

Ronnie didn't say anything else.

Green couldn't let it end there. "Are you saying you might be queer?" they asked. "Or LGBTQIAP+ in some way? I mean"—Green paused—"well, some of the letters anyway. I mean, you're not L." Green gasped. "Are you?"

"Nah." Ronnie grinned. "One of my moms is a lesbian, but it's not my style. I guess I'm not really in a space to put words on it." He shrugged. "I've always liked girls before . . ."

"Before?" Green's eyes and heart grew wide.

"I just mean I don't want to limit myself. I'd think you, of all people, would get that."

"Oh," said Green, holding a sigh in their throat. "Well, thanks for asking me to join crew."

"Glad you joined!" If Ronnie noticed how disappointed Green was, he didn't show it.

Green and Ronnie joined the group forming around Ms. Jones. She congratulated them on their efficiency and hoped they would all be back next week.

Once everyone was ready, Ms. Jones and Mr. Sydney walked with the cast and crew to the main school doors. Green found themself in a conversation with Dini about how excited he was to play a wizard in the play. Maybe he could even do a magic trick onstage.

Green tried to get back into conversation with Ronnie, but he was already chatting with Melissa and Leila, and soon the whole bunch was chatting as one. Green's questions remained unformed and unspoken.

Green tried all week to ask Ronnie more about him *not wanting to limit himself*, but it was tough. Green didn't want to sound rude, and they certainly didn't want to tell Ronnie why it mattered without knowing the answer. They tried to bring it up indirectly, by talking about how Miss Kris had said that she was *at least a little bit gay*, but either Ronnie didn't realize what they were doing, or he did realize it and was avoiding talking about his own maybe-not-straightness, because he immediately steered the conversation back to working on the play.

Green got close to asking at the beginning of lunch one day, but then Rick showed up and the question evaporated into the air. It was probably for the best, because if the conversation had gone wrong, it would have been the most awkward lunch period ever.

Eventually, it had been too long since Ronnie's original comment, and Green thought it would sound like they had been thinking about it too much. Which they had. So they didn't say anything else about it. But they couldn't help feeling that maybe, if they could figure out when to bring it up, it would go just right. Maybe it didn't matter what Ronnie called himself . . . but it *did* matter who he liked.

## ★ CHAPTER XI ★

# ICE CREAM BREAK

That weekend, Dad went upstairs to help Lulu with her yearly book cull, when she looked through her shelves and donated old reads to make space for new books. Dad usually came home with a big stack of thick fantasy novels for himself and at least a few graphic novels for Green, which he added to piles on top of and in front of their many overflowing bookcases. Dad said he was happy to help Lulu abandon her word children if that was her wish, but that he would keep his pals of prose and poetry by his side.

It was Green's job to keep Kandy and Randey occupied while they worked. Kandy and Randey might be a handful, but they were a handful Green understood.

They didn't even know about crushes, much less what it meant to have a crush on a boy who might be straight but didn't want to *limit* himself.

Kandy and Randey came trampling down the stairs and flanked Green, who was trying to ignore Ronnie's smile in their mind by rereading an internet recipe.

"Whatcha doing?" they asked in singsong unison. Green had once told them it was creepy when they did that, so now they did it whenever they came over, no matter how many times Green ignored it.

Instead, Green asked, "Do you know what ice cream is made of?"

"Cream!" announced Randey.

"And ice!" declared Kandy.

"Pretty much!" Green pulled a bowl of ice out of the freezer and a pint of heavy cream out of the fridge. They placed them far back on the counter, out of reach of Kandy and Randey, even on the step stools that Kandy and Randey were already pulling over.

"Plus sugar and flavor." Green added the sugar and vanilla extract to the counter, along with a measuring cup and spoon.

"Are we gonna make ice cream?" asked Kandy.

"We sure are!" They were proud of having thought of such a cool activity to do with Kandy and Randey, and for thinking of it early enough to ask Dad to buy the cream.

"But don't you need, like, a big machine to freeze it?" asked Randey.

"Yeah," said Kandy. "When they make ice cream on cooking shows, they always fight to get to the machine."

Green held up a few sealable plastic bags and a carton of salt. "Meet the world's simplest ice cream machine."

"Really?" asked Kandy and Randey, as one. This time, they weren't trying to be creepy. They were just twins.

"Really!" said Green. At least, they hoped so. They

had watched a few YouTube videos where it worked, but they hadn't ever tried it before.

They opened the carton of cream and handed it to Kandy, who poured the thick liquid into the glass measuring cup. Green measured sugar and vanilla for Randey to add, then stirred the contents until the sugar dissolved. For a moment, they wondered whether Ronnie liked ice cream, then literally shook the idea from their mind, their green hair flopping back and forth.

"It's not fair," said Kandy. "We're making Randey's favorite. Why can't we make bubble gum flavor? That's *my* favorite."

Green was glad for the distraction, even for an *it's not fair* moment. "I have no idea how to make bubble gum flavor. Do you?"

The twins shook their heads.

"Then, vanilla it is."

"Remember that time you made us taste the vanilla by itself?" said Kandy.

"I didn't *make* you taste it," they said too innocently. "I offered and you agreed."

"But you knew it was disgusting!" said Randey.

"River was over, and the three of you wouldn't leave me alone," Green said in their defense. "Besides, it was funny!"

They laughed, remembering the contortions of the younger kids' faces. Green had been getting ready to make a batch of chocolate chip cookies to pull themself out of a bad mood. Meanwhile, Randey, Kandy, and River were running in and out of the kitchen, taking turns crouching on the ground and then popping up and screaming when another of them came in the room. It was like a game of hide-and-seek where the goal was to find the seeker. A loud, annoying, twisted game of hide-and-seek. And after every round, they would demand to know when the cookies would be ready. So Green had decided to encourage them to play elsewhere.

They opened the bottle of vanilla, and waved it under six tiny nostrils, so that the thick, warm notes filled their scent receptors. Notes that you would think would be sweet, especially if you're a kid who has only had vanilla in snacks and desserts. But notes that are not at all sweet if they haven't yet been combined with sugar. Notes which are terribly bitter and unpleasant if you are unwise enough to imbibe the elixir directly, which is what all three children had done.

Green drew the bottle by their noses twice more, then pulled out a spoon and worked quickly. Left to right, Green brought the spoon to each of their lips and let them take a taste. While Randey's face started to contort, Green moved on to Kandy, and by the time Randey had recovered enough control to warn River, both River and Kandy were sticking their tongues out of their mouths in a desperate attempt to get away from the awfulness, but as their taste buds were on their tongues, it hadn't helped.

Green had tossed an ice pop at each of them to keep them from complaining to the adults, and then threatened that none of them would get any cookies if they didn't leave Green alone.

But that was when Green had been in a bad mood. Mostly Green liked hanging out with little kids, even ones who were practically siblings. That might not be cool to say, but cool had never been Green's goal. Unless, of course, ice cream was involved.

Being Kid-in-Charge meant they got to lead activities. Plus, proving to your dad that you were responsible had its advantages, like having flexible wind-down guidelines instead of a firm bedtime. That meant that as long as Green woke up in the morning without complaining, and they weren't too loud at night, it didn't really matter what time they went to sleep.

Green gave Kandy and Randey each a gallon-sized plastic bag, took one for themself, and showed how to fill them with ice. They added salt to each bag and set them aside. Then Green gave Kandy and Randey each a pint-sized locking plastic storage bag and told them to hold them tight while Green poured a third of the mixture into each bag, then poured one for themself. Green sealed all three small bags carefully, and put each into another small bag before putting them into the ice bags.

"Now we squish them around," Green announced.

Randey laid the bag on the counter and punched it right in the middle.

"Not too hard, you goof!" said Green. "You don't want to make a hole in the plastic or you'll end up with super-salty ice cream."

Kandy and Randey made identical faces of disgust.

"And that's if you're lucky," Green added. "You could also end up with no ice cream at all and a giant mess to clean up."

Kandy poked at the corner of her bag with her pinkie until Green said, "You can go a little harder than that."

Green, Kandy, and Randey started shaking their bags in rhythm, and soon all three of them were dancing around, inventing and copying cool arm moves as the sweetened cream got colder and thicker. They were gathered in a tiny conga line, using their bags as maracas, when Dad came in. He dropped a trilogy of thick paperbacks with worn spines on a pile of books by the door and picked up a cardboard box he had meant to bring up earlier.

"I see you three are keeping busy," said Dad.

"We're making ice cream!" yelled Kandy and Randey.

"Yum!" Dad smacked his lips. "Did you make enough for me too?"

"Oh," said Green, who hadn't been expecting Dad to come back down until after the ice cream was eaten. "I . . . I could share mine . . . I guess."

Dad chuckled. "I'm just messing with you. Lulu and I have snacks upstairs, and we're ordering pizza for dinner. Have fun. And make sure you clean up when you're done." He waved his hand over the general mess the kitchen had become before returning upstairs. Even though Green had tried to be careful, there were still drops of cream, not only on the counter, but also on the sink, floor, and even the freezer door. At least the ceiling was still clean.

Green checked their bag and the ice cream had firmed up wonderfully. Kandy's and Randey's were still pretty soupy, so Green directed them in cleaning up the cream spots and putting away the ingredients while giving the bags some extra high-speed shakes. Green grabbed some spoons, and headed out to the porch, Kandy and Randey at their heels.

"Ooooooh," said Kandy as Green unwrapped her inner bag, now filled with fresh ice cream.

"Ahhhhhh," said Randey as Green opened his.

"Ohhhhhh," said Green, revealing their own dairy treat. They put in their spoon and took a bite. Perfect. Sweet, cold, and creamy. They ate together, quiet except for the occasional exclamation of epicurean joy. The vanilla danced on their taste buds, and the sweet cream coated their tongues as they licked every last drop.

Green sent Kandy and Randey upstairs to wash and change their shirts while Green rinsed the outer bags to be used again. They hated to toss any plastic in the trash, but the inner bags were such a sticky mess that it would take a bunch of soap and water to clean them, and Dad said that at that point, it was hard to say whether it was environmentally worth doing.

They picked up one of the graphic novels Dad had

gotten from Lulu and went back onto the porch to read about a dragon and a princess who were best friends, but big muscled guys kept trying to rescue the princess and ruining their picnic plans.

Or, at least, they tried to read. Mostly, they thought about Ronnie. How he smiled. How he laughed. How he smelled just a little bit sweet, like honey and coconut. But mostly, how mind-bendingly baffling he was to a simple queer nonbinary kid like Green.

# CHAPTER XII

# IT'S NOT EASY BEING GREEN

Plays took a lot of practice and preparation. Melissa, Tracey, and other actors with songs and lots of lines had been meeting with Mr. Sydney on Mondays and Wednesdays, based on the scenes they were in. The band met on Mondays and Wednesdays as well. Thursdays, of course, were reserved for Rainbow Spectrum meetings, and not even Melissa wanted to rehearse on Fridays. And every Tuesday, the full cast gathered, along with the crew.

Mr. Sydney rolled up his red shirtsleeves, loosed his red plaid bow tie, and gathered the group. They started each meeting in a big circle that barely fit onstage. Everyone did warm-ups, even the crew. Even Ms. Jones. Green thought they were the best part of rehearsal. Maybe even better than spending time with Ronnie. Maybe.

They shook their legs *two-three-four-five-six-seven-eight*, hands *two-three-four*, shoulders *two*, head. They made big sounds and little sounds, took big steps and little steps. They made alien noises, fought off imaginary attack hamsters, and pretended to be in a windstorm, a desert, and on the surface of the moon. The more dramatic the scene, the sillier they got, and most warm-ups ended up with at least half the cast and crew on the floor in fits of laughter.

"And with that," said Ms. Jones, approaching the circle, "we've got to be going. It's a big build day and there's no time to waste. We have additional help today, and we don't want to keep them waiting."

Ms. Jones led her group out to the blacktop yard, where long strips of wood lay in stacks next to paint cans, brushes, and a set of tarps. The crew had decided to build a cool new boxlike contraption for the Wizard to stand behind, instead of being offstage as in past years, and a real platform for Dorothy to find the Scarecrow on, instead of a step stool.

"You said someone was coming to help us?" asked Brinley, looking around the empty yard. Today she wore an oversized black sweatshirt, bright pink leggings covered in tiny sharks, and yellow high-top sneakers.

"I certainly did," Ms. Jones answered. "And here they come!"

She pointed down the block where half a dozen teenagers and a teacher were walking over from Levithan High School. The students were carrying large black bags in addition to their book bags. The teacher was shorter and slimmer than most of the students, but her gait, clipboard, and placement at the front of the group made her position clear. She had short graying hair that was white at the temples, leathery skin, and wore a blue button-down shirt with a name tag that said *Sparky*.

Three of the students had brightly colored hair: one with a single streak of pink, another with long, deep blue, curling locs, and a third with short hair every color of the rainbow and then some, including probably Atomic Alligator. Green wondered how long it must have taken them to get their hair like that. The one time they'd tried adding some Lucky Lime to their hair, it had taken Lulu an hour and a bunch of aluminum foil to apply it, and in the end, it had looked like crabgrass.

Once the group arrived, Ms. Jones introduced them as the senior woodworking class and their teacher, Ms. Feinberg.

Ronnie waved at a tall kid with endless dark ringlets that hung past his shoulders, and the beginnings of a mustache across his pale, white face.

"You know him?" Green asked.

"That's Melissa's brother, Scott."

Green waved too, and Scott waved back.

"Thank you so much for joining us, Ms. Feinberg." The group turned to Ms. Jones as she spoke.

"Happy to be here and to bring my star builders," Ms. Feinberg said with a robust voice and a sharp smile.

"Yeah, we need the community service credit," said a thick kid who looked like he could be a football linebacker . . . because he *was* a football linebacker.

"There's that," said Ms. Feinberg, turning to her students. "But also this is a great experience for you all, some of whom might want to get into set design someday." She turned back to the middle schoolers. "Now, I want to be clear that my students have been instructed in how to carefully and appropriately use the woodworking tools they have brought here today. The only people who should be touching any of them are my students and myself, and everyone should be wearing protective goggles if they are within twenty feet of anyone working with them."

"Then what are we even here for?" asked Kadyn.

"We're gonna need you to hand us the nails," said the high schooler with rainbow hair.

"Are we allowed to do *that*?" asked Brinley, holding her face in an exaggerated question mark.

"Yes," said Ms. Jones. "You can hand over nails, but you are not to hold them in place when a hammer is swinging at them. We don't need to risk any accidents."

"My students know that the only hand who should be holding their nail is their own," said Ms. Feinberg with a smile. "But we certainly need your help making measurements, holding wood steady, and keeping track of the directions. There's plenty for you to do."

"Alright then, crew," said Ms. Jones. "Let's make good use of our volunteers' time and see how much we can get done this afternoon!"

She laid out the goals for the day and announced that there would be three teams. Team A would build a structure for the Wizard to hide behind, while Team B would carve designs to attach to the base to make it look even cooler. Team C would make the Scarecrow's platform.

Kadyn joined her friends Victor and Cindy on Team A. Brinley and Violet, who loved art, signed up for Team B. That left Ronnie and Green on Team C. Making a platform was less exciting than making a Wizard's hideout, perhaps, but the company couldn't be beat.

Green and Ronnie were soon joined by Scott and the linebacker kid, who introduced himself as Mac. They opened their bags, which were filled with hammers, saws, rulers, and plenty of tools Green didn't know the names of, along with safety goggles, tarps, and other protective gear.

"Wow," said Ronnie. "They sure do trust you with the sharp objects."

Green couldn't decide whose grin was goofier, Scott's or Mac's, but Scott handed out goggles, saying, "It is extremely important that you wear them while we're working."

"Yeah," said Mac, "if you don't, and Ms. Feinberg sees, we'll be in serious trouble."

Their attitudes might have been silly, but they treated their tools seriously, examining each one before laying it out on a towel, like they were surgeons.

Ms. Feinberg came by with a nod and a set of instructions. To start, they needed to cut the wood, which meant that Ronnie and Green needed to measure it so that Scott and Mac could do the actual cutting. Ronnie stretched the measuring tape down the length of the plank and Green stood by with a pencil to mark where Ronnie held the ruler.

The directions made the project sound more complicated than it was, but once Green looked at the diagrams, they could see it was simple. They just needed to run some slats across a base with cross-bracing to handle the weight of the actor standing on it.

"See," Green explained, showing where the bracing created triangles. "This is why it works. Triangles are the strongest shape!"

"Even the ones that are acute?" Ronnie grinned.

"Oh, don't be obtuse." Green grinned back.

"You're just saying I'm right," said Ronnie, and they both laughed.

"At least it's not as bad as being straight."

Ronnie didn't laugh at that one.

The air around Green sank thick and heavy onto their shoulders. "I'm sorry. It's just, you're the one who said you were a cis het guy. But you also don't want to limit yourself."

Green knew they should stop there, but weeks of waiting patiently cracked all at once and washed over them like a wave of fire. "So, which is it? Are you straight or not?" The question felt like a missile, and Green didn't even feel bad about launching it.

"Does it matter?" Ronnie shrugged.

Green couldn't tell whether he didn't care, or whether he wanted to look like he didn't care. Either way, it was infuriating.

Green's voice calmed, even if their insides still boiled. "I mean, it kinda does."

"It's just a label."

"Yeah, a label that means that you only like girls."

"I know that."

"And either you do or you don't."

"It's just . . . it's complicated, okay?"

"It's really not, though. If . . ." Green could hear

the words *you like me* in their head, but they couldn't say them out loud. Or wouldn't. The answer could be no, and that would be even worse than Ronnie saying he was straight.

"If . . . ?" Ronnie echoed.

"Nevermind," said Green. Ronnie was right. It was terribly complicated.

"Hey!" said Scott. "Less arguing and more measuring."

Green bristled. They hadn't been arguing. They had just been . . . disagreeing. Ronnie had the same thought written across his face, but neither of them could appreciate it. Instead, as they got back to measuring and drawing, they purposefully looked at the wood, the ground, Scott, Mac, the sky. Anything but each other's faces.

# ★ CHAPTER XIII ★

# GREEN SEES RED

Green practiced juggling after Saturday's pancake breakfast, and thought about how it was a lot easier to juggle smoothly when things were already going well. Once one ball was out of alignment, everything else usually got worse and soon you were giving up and starting over. Life was sort of like that, except that you couldn't start over. You just had to keep going, even if you knew you were throwing out of control.

They had felt out of control when they had flat-out demanded Ronnie label himself. But there was nothing they could do about it. Maybe they could say something to him next week, but for now they were looking for anything to take their mind off it. So when Nana asked them whether they'd like to go get pizza and go grocery shopping, Green agreed happily.

The double-Z Nana signed reminded Green of the way the smell of yeast and grease filled the air at Sammy's. They had the best pie in town, and they were across the street from Joanne's, Nana's favorite grocery store.

Green stashed their juggling balls in their room and slipped into their sneakers.

One of the great things about riding in the car with Nana was that she didn't hear the radio, so Green could put on whatever song they wanted at whatever volume they felt like. If the music was so loud that the car vibrated, Nana just laughed and turned up the bass, so that the car really shook, and the two of them seat-danced to the beat.

Nana pulled into the parking lot for Sammy's and

soon they were toasting each other with the tips of their slices. Green took a bite and the cheese stretched back to the plate. They twirled the thinning strand around their tongue until it finally snapped.

When they were done and had wiped the grease off their hands, they crossed the street to Joanne's. It was older and smaller than the supermarket Dad usually went to, but Nana liked it there because one of the people who worked at the deli signed, and sometimes she would order a pound of ham or potato salad, just to say hi to "my friend Bob."

But that day, Bob wasn't behind the counter, so they went to the prepackaged meats. Nana could speak English when she needed to, and there was always pen and paper, not to mention Green to interpret, but she said it was nicer not to have to bother with explaining yourself to people. Green could relate.

As Nana picked through the potatoes, Green was hit with the need to pee. Suddenly and sharply. They grumbled at their choice of a large root beer and hoped the feeling would pass. Peeing in public meant using a public bathroom. They followed Nana down the condiments aisle and squeezed their legs together tightly as she mulled over honey mustard salad dressing.

They followed Nana with small, careful steps, but when she stopped again to decide on a pasta shape, Green knew they wouldn't make it to the end of the store, much less all the way home. They tapped their grandmother on the shoulder and waved a *T* in the air to let her know they were headed to the toilet. They hurried past the pasta sauces and pickles, pretty sure it was already too late. Their thighs felt wet as they slipped against each other.

At the front of the store, to the left of the customer

service desk, was a short hallway, and at the end of that short hallway were two doors with Line Guy and Triangle Woman. Darn. Green had been hoping for a family stall. Luckily, they were singles, at least. The women's room was occupied, with a red circle next to the handle, so Green slipped into the men's.

They stumbled to the toilet, already pulling down their pants, and peed so hard and long they felt dizzy. Closing their eyes, they rested their head on their hand, which was itself resting on the toilet paper roll. They took a deep breath, and then another, as if there hadn't been room in their body for air before. They opened their eyes to a big red splotch in their underwear. Worse, the toilet bowl water was orangey pink.

It had happened. They had known it would happen, but they thought they would be at home. There was already a pack of pads in the bottom drawer in the bathroom for *when the day came.*

But here they were, in the grocery store men's room, showerless and padless. Their underwear was a bloody, sticky mess and who knew how much more was coming before they made it home. They wrapped a few layers of thin toilet paper around their underwear and bunched up a wad on top of that. When they stood, there was a red smear at the front of the toilet seat, which they wiped down. They could already feel the paper shifting around between their legs as they washed their hands.

They tried to tell themself it wasn't a big deal. It was a natural bodily function, and they hadn't bled through their jeans or anything super embarrassing. They had started growing a chest at the end of sixth grade, and that hadn't bothered them. This was no different.

But it was a big deal. And it was different. Green didn't have to *do* anything when they started growing except tell Lulu they weren't interested in shopping for bras. But they had just washed their own blood off their hands and their underbelly hurt, like someone was pressing a butter knife lengthwise against their pelvis. And knowing that most of it technically wasn't blood didn't help. The idea of *shedding their uterine lining* was way grosser than blood.

They hoped that the toilet paper mess they had left in their pants would hold until Nana was done shopping and went back to find her already at the freezers.

"Everything okay?" Nana asked.

"Yeah." Green wasn't sure whether they were okay, but they had no intention of starting a conversation about periods with Nana in the middle of the grocery store.

After Nana dropped them off at home, Green ran immediately to the bathroom, stripped off their clothing, and got into the shower as soon as it was warm enough to bear. They scrubbed their legs and ran water between them, then soaped up their body and slowly turned around as the hot water steamed and cleaned them.

Standing outside the shower afterward, wrapped in a towel, they weren't sure what to do next. They didn't want to get blood on the towel, so they used some toilet paper, and sure enough, it came back bright red. They pulled the package of pads from under the sink, tore through the plastic to grab one, and dashed to their room.

The back of the pad didn't seem very sticky, but it stayed in place once Green pulled up their underpants. They finished getting dressed, stuffing their blood-stained clothing in the closet to deal with later, and washed their hands again.

Green scrolled through the music app on their phone and tapped on the image of a hellish red sunset over a cemetery, with creepy hands hovering in the air, and between them the lightning-like band logo with its iconic *M* and *A*. Metallica's third album, *Master of Puppets.*

Slow, eerie guitar emanated from speakers that hung from the four corners of their room. Green raised the volume as the notes repeated, with a second guitar adding harmony. Suddenly, the sound burst open, wide and loud, with the same driving beat.

Green's body filled with energy. They bounced in place with the swift rhythm, and by the time the guitar ramped into the first verse, they were thrashing their head up and down like they'd seen in videos. They grinned when they noticed their hair flying in and out of view, and imagined what it would be like in a mosh pit, bouncing into people as they carved out space to let loose.

Metallica songs were long, so by the time the charging guitar faded away, Green was sweating, breathing a little heavy, and a bit dizzy, but the next song started with a set of crisp chords that set Green's body back into motion. They flailed their arms, their head, their legs to the rhythm. They couldn't make out many of the words beyond the chanted *Master* that the lead singer, James Hetfield, growled about, but his raw voice made it clear that you didn't want to be under their control.

One of the great things about Metallica was that none of their songs were about love or relationships or any of that stuff that most bands sang about. Well, a couple were, but not many, and none in their earlier, shoutier albums. Green felt good to know they weren't unwillingly headbanging to some heteronormative love story or, worse, some song about women's bodies being hot like pie, which was more than you could say for most music.

On the fade-out, Green acted like a marionette, dancing as though someone were pulling strings attached to their limbs. As the song drifted into maniacal laughter, they crumpled on the ground and let the slow, creepy opening to "The Thing That Should Not Be" wash over them.

That's when Dad knocked on the door.

"Yeah?"

"Can I come in?"

"Sure."

Dad stood in the doorway, banging his head slightly. He took in the sight of Green, arms splayed, one knee bent in the air. Green, curious why Dad hadn't said anything, opened their eyes.

Dad waved. "Killer, hunh?"

"They're pretty cool." Green was highly aware that Dad was proud that his kid listened to what he called "his" music, which Green thought was kind of funny because Dad couldn't play a note on anything but a kazoo. And then they thought about Dad playing the opening harmonic notes of "Welcome Home (Sanitarium)" on a kazoo and they let out a giggle.

"What's so funny?" Dad asked, so Green told him about the image in their head, and Dad laughed too.

"Mind if I join you?" Dad gestured at the floor next to Green.

"Sure." Green shrugged, which was surprisingly hard to do effectively while lying down.

"The Mighty Met, man," Dad said once he settled in, fingers laced like a pillow behind his head. "You can't beat 'em. I mean, plenty of bands were heavier, but no one constructed a song like those guys. Like they were writing eight symphonies an album."

"Aren't they still around?" Green folded their arms behind their head, mirroring Dad.

"Yeah, but something changed after they lost Cliff." Cliff Burton, the band's original bassist, had been killed in a bus crash in 1986. "Don't get me wrong. Rob Trujillo is a legend. But those early albums? There's nothing like 'em."

Green and Dad lay side by side as they listened.

"I used to play it loud like this," said Dad, after the driving chorus where James pleaded to be left alone faded back into a mournful guitar riff. "Especially when I had something I was working through in my head. It was good to drown out my thoughts for a little bit."

Dad had this funny way of asking a question without asking a question. Green liked it. It made it easier not to answer if you didn't feel like it. Or if you needed a few more minutes to get your thoughts in order after having banged your brain around in your skull for fifteen minutes.

"I had long hair when I was younger, you know," Dad said, changing the topic before the silence got too heavy.

"I know."

"It was even longer than yours before you cut it," Dad bragged.

"You told me that when I did it," said Green. Dad had said that a person could have long hair and not be a girl, and had pulled out old photos of him hanging out with his high school friends, most of them with long hair and wearing plaid, unbuttoned shirts over band tees, with ripped jeans and heavy, black boots. Green had been unconvinced and had gotten most of it nearly buzzed anyway, except for the wave at the front that hung just short of their eyes.

"There's a lot of different ways of expressing your gender, and lots of things that people think are about gender but aren't actually at all."

"Uh, yeah, Dad, I know."

Okay, so Dad would shift the topic, rather than change it entirely, but still, it bought Green a few minutes. They lay on the ground together, tapping their fingers and toes in time with the power chords that drove the song along.

The next track started. Green didn't know the name of it. That happened a lot with Metallica, especially for the first minute or two, before James started singing. But it was fast and powerful, and it helped push the words off their tongue.

"Dad, can I tell you about something that happened?"

Green sat up cross-legged on the floor. Dad joined them, face-to-face.

"Always. I love you no matter what you do." He stretched over and turned down the stereo so that they could talk more easily.

"It's not something I *did*, really." Green grimaced.

"Or what someone else does to you. I'm here for you, buddy."

"It wasn't someone else either."

"Well, now I'm curious."

Green paused, which made it seem like a big deal,

which was the last thing they wanted to have be true. Even if it was. And then the pause grew longer as they realized they didn't really know what words to use. *Menstruation* was too scientific, and *that time of the month* sounded like what an old person would say. They kind of wanted to just say that they were bleeding, but they weren't sure Dad would understand what they meant.

"I got my period." Green was relieved that the words had escaped their mouth.

"Oh!" Dad sounded startled.

"Should I talk to Lulu?" Green asked with a wince. Even though Green wasn't a girl, it was a girl problem. Wasn't it?

"No, it's just, to be honest, I sort of forgot that was going to happen."

"Me too," said Green. They both laughed.

"No, wait." Green paused, as if listening to their

own thought once more before sharing it. "It's not that I forgot. It's more that I didn't believe it."

"Oh?" Dad asked in his way that meant, *say more about that.*

"Like, I know my body is AFAB," said Green, which stood for *Assigned Female At Birth.* "And I know I'm not on blockers. So, I probably shouldn't have been surprised, but I still was."

"Can I ask when it started?"

"Sometime after I left the house with Nana."

"Did you tell her?"

Green shook their head.

"Well, I'm sure she would have been fine, but it's your information to share. Or not. I'm glad you told me though. Sometimes sharing a piece of news can help it feel real."

"I'm not sure I want it to feel real."

"Well, that's its own jar of pickles," said Dad. After

a pause, he asked, "Does it bother you? That you have your period?"

Green shivered at the word. "Yeah, sorta. I guess."

Dad prompted for more with another, "Oh?"

"I mean, it feels kinda gross, for one."

"Are you sore?"

"A little bit."

"There's pain relievers in the bathroom if you need them."

"I don't think so," said Green. "At least not right now. Mostly, it feels kinda, well, slimy and yucky."

"I'll take your word for it," said Dad, making a slightly unpleasant face.

"But also it's like, *Welcome to Womanhood!*" Green grinned with mock enthusiasm and flashed sarcastic jazz hands.

"Well, now hold on a minute there, my young headbanger."

"Are you going to be Ally Dad, telling me that since it's my body, nothing about it is a woman's?"

"I mean, you're not wrong," said Dad.

"It sure feels like my body hasn't picked up on the nonbinary memo."

"Maybe. But maybe that's cisgender normativity taking residence in your head."

Green perked up. They loved when cisgender anything was to blame, especially when they weren't the one to point it out. Just because it was common, or *normative*, that people who menstruated were women didn't mean that everyone was, or that they were better somehow. It's just that there were so many cisgender people, and most people assumed everyone was cisgender.

"Anyway, I know, talking with your dad about body stuff isn't cool."

"It's not *too* bad," said Green. "I mean, it's not awesome, but . . . thanks, Dad." Having their period wasn't great, but Green was glad they had Dad to talk to about it, and to remind them that it didn't change who they were.

"Anytime, my little Green Bean." Dad pulled out a handful of wrapped chocolate pieces and laid them on the floor. "Here. If Lulu is right, you'll want those."

"I do!" Green unwrapped two and put them in their mouth at once. They had always loved chocolate, but they weren't sure it had ever tasted quite this good.

"Wait," Green asked, after popping a third piece into their mouth. "Do you just walk around with chocolates in your pocket?"

"Only when I hear my favorite kid blasting my favorite band." Dad grinned and stood with a grunt. On the way out the door, he punched the volume back up. "Orion," he said, naming the instrumental that had started. "You're gonna wanna lay back down and close your eyes for this one. Let it take you places."

Dad closed the door on the way out, and Green sailed through the notes as they left their body and thoughts behind.

# CHAPTER XIV

# YOU MADE YOUR BED, NOW SULK IN IT

By Tuesday, Green wouldn't say that they were used to the feeling of a pad between their legs, but it had stopped surprising them every time they went to the bathroom. They didn't love having their period, but they wouldn't call it the worst thing to happen. It wasn't even the worst thing to happen that week, which was not chatting and laughing with Ronnie.

Ronnie and Green had been friendly enough since the last crew meeting, but they hadn't really talked. In English class, Green made sure that their bag was packed and ready to go before the bell rang so that they could be out of the room before Ronnie even stood up, and they made sure to get to the lunch table late every day so that they wouldn't have to spend time alone together. It was a lonely, scheming week. And the worst part was, if they had been scheming *with* Ronnie instead of *about* him, it probably would have been fun.

During rehearsal warm-ups, they made sure not to stand next to Ronnie, and when it was their turn with the imaginary ball, they didn't throw it his way, even though they wanted to.

"Are we working outside again?" Ronnie asked Ms. Jones once warm-ups were done.

"Not today. We're heading to the gym so we can lay the fabric out. It finally arrived in the mail!" There were only two weeks left until the play, and the crew still needed to make the flying-pig costumes.

"We're sewing?" Green's face looked like they had smelled something rotten. Lulu had tried to teach them to sew once, and it was a mess. Their seams zigzagged back and forth, and sometimes they sewed right off the fabric.

"I'm not sure how else you expect us to make flying-pig costumes," said Ms. Jones. "But don't worry, Ms. Feinberg's class is coming again to help."

The gym was surprisingly quiet as the crew entered. Usually the echoey room was filled with the squeaks of sneakers and the thumps of rubber balls pounding on the ground, but today there was a heavy bolt of pink fabric leaning against the wall, near the door, and a large bag that spelled out *Ms. Jones's Sewing Bag* in a patchwork of bright fabrics on a black background. Green wondered how many seams it must have taken to sew that bag.

Ms. Jones directed the crew to the classroom next door to get desks and chairs, and by the time they had set them up in the gym, Ms. Feinberg and her students had joined them. Scott, Mac, and the others carried sturdy black boxes to the tables and opened them to reveal sewing machines.

"Lightweight portable models," Ms. Feinberg said to Ms. Jones with pride.

Soon, there were large rectangles of pink fabric all over the gym floor, and each member of the crew was teamed up with a high schooler to pin see-through-thin pattern pieces onto the fabric.

Green was assigned to work with Scott. Ronnie worked with the kid with blue locs on the other side of the auditorium. Green couldn't decide whether they were disappointed or relieved not to be working with Ronnie. They couldn't avoid him forever. And even if they could, they didn't want to.

They were still staring Ronnie's way when he looked their direction. They flinched, nearly knocking over the open box of pins.

"Watch what you're doing!" said Scott. "Remember, *safety first, second, and third.*" They adopted Ms.

Feinberg's husky voice, but with a smile that suggested respect rather than derision.

Once they were finished pinning, Scott showed Green how to hold the fabric tight and the scissors wide to make a smooth cut. "Now, you do that for the rest while I get the sewing machine set up."

Amid the clatter of sewing machines and scissors, Green didn't notice the gym door open at first, but they certainly noticed when Principal Baker approached Ms. Jones with a trio of kids—Jeff and two of his friends, Lee and Jarrett.

"Well, who do we have here?" said Ms. Jones, though she clearly knew who all three were.

"Seems these three have earned themselves detention," said Principal Baker. "And I was thinking it would be a shame for them to sit in my office, wasting time, when they could be of service to the community."

"That's a lovely idea," Ms. Jones said. "We have

a lot going on today, and we could certainly use the help.

"I'll be just down the hall if you run into any difficulties. I can always take them back for silent detention if necessary." Principal Baker turned to the boys and added, "Don't make it necessary," before heading back inside.

Ms. Jones turned to the three boys. "We'll be glad to have your help today."

"You can't make us do work." Jeff's sneer filled his face. "Detention just means you have to sit there."

"You are most certainly welcome to sit silently against the wall."

"But there are no chairs there. You want me to sit on the *ground*?" Jeff scoffed.

"You do it every day in gym class," Ms. Jones said with a smile that was wearing thin.

"That's in my gym shorts. These are my new pants!"

Green didn't know how teachers dealt with kids

who were like that. They wanted to scream *You sit with your friends on the playground every day, you hypocrite.* But teachers had to act nice. Or, at least, they had to act like it didn't bother them.

Ms. Jones handed him a scrap of fabric to sit on without a word. Jeff refused it, mumbling something about pink being worse than dirt.

Jeff turned to Lee and Jarrett with a "C'mon guys," but neither followed him.

"Can we talk if we help?" Lee asked Ms. Jones.

Ms. Jones smiled. "As long as you're productive, I don't see why a little conversation isn't acceptable."

"Sweet!" said Jarrett. He and Lee high-fived as Jeff scowled.

Ms. Jones gave the two boys the job of going around and picking up scraps of fabric scattered around the gym so that no one slipped.

"You know you're picking up trash for trash," Jeff said to Lee as he passed.

"Best detention ever!" said Lee with a grin.

"Lee!" Ms. Jones called from across the room. "You may talk, but you may *not* talk to Jeff. Jeff has chosen a more traditional punishment. If I see you over there again, both of you will be back in Principal Baker's office immediately."

"Wait, that's Jeff?" said Scott.

"You know Jeff?" asked Green.

"Let's just say I've heard of him before." Scott shot him a look that said that he would rather never hear of him again.

When all four sewing machines were chunking and revving, the room was so loud that you had to yell to be heard. Green was surprised to find that not only did they not hate sewing in a group, but they were actually pretty good at it. Okay, they were good at pinning and cutting, but Scott said those were the hard parts, really.

"Sewing a straight line just takes practice," Scott said.

"For me to do something straight?" said Green. "Yeah, that'll take a lot of practice."

"Good one!" said Scott with a laugh.

Green grinned, proud of their joke and trying not to think about whether Ronnie would like it or think that they were saying something negative about straight people.

By the time the afternoon was done, the pile of fabric had turned into six winged-pig costumes, and one of them was the one Green and Scott had made. Green hadn't sewn a straight seam, but they hadn't had to. And they hadn't worked with Ronnie, but it had been fun anyway. Maybe this was what Mr. Sydney meant when he talked about the magic of theater. Still, though, it would have been even more fun if they had been able to smile at Ronnie from across the room instead of worrying that he was looking their way.

Green couldn't help feeling the tiniest bit like Jeff. Sure, they weren't sitting off by themself and stewing, but they also weren't laughing with Ronnie. And sure, Jeff was sitting alone because he couldn't get over himself enough to have a good time. But then again, worrying so much about Ronnie that they weren't having fun together didn't sound so different.

# CHAPTER XV

# BEING WHO YOU ARE

Green had mostly stopped bleeding after four days, but they wore a pad for another week, just in case. Lulu said that things could be spotty at first, and she was right. There were a few drops that weekend.

It was the same yuck that Lulu dealt with, and half the population of the world, really. And it was the yuck that made babies possible. But that didn't make it any less yucky, at least not to Green. And if it was supposed to come every month, it was never much more than three weeks away. Lulu said that some people who menstruated celebrated their connection to the moon, and that she had been part of some meaningful ceremonies when she was in her late teens, but that it was also okay to find the whole thing unpleasant.

Dad had put a bottle of pain relievers out in the bathroom, but Green wasn't in pain, after a bit of achiness that first weekend. They were at least glad for that. It was more that their body felt weird, which, when Green thought about it, was probably true for a lot of cisgender people when they got their first periods too. Sudden blood is weird. There were even kids from conservative families who didn't know periods existed. That must have been scary. At least they knew it was coming. But Green was still on Team Unpleasant.

Green had done a little more reading about hormone blockers. They would stop your period, but they would also stop your body from developing in other ways, and Green couldn't say for sure that they wanted that. They enjoyed the small curves they were starting to see on their body, and they didn't necessarily want those to stop.

Between that and not even knowing what *straight* was anymore, Green was confused. They needed to confer with someone who understood these things.

Once again, Green found themself heading after Rainbow Spectrum toward the stop for a bus they didn't take, but this time, it wasn't to see how close they could walk next to Ronnie without actually touching them. They didn't approach Ronnie at all, who was deep in conversation with Rick anyway. There was someone else they wanted to talk with.

"Hey, Melissa. Could I ask you about something?" Green had meant to sound casual, but the words came out in capitalized, bold font and hung in the air, the word *something* encircled with flashing Broadway marquee lights.

Melissa scrunched her face slightly and asked, "About you or about me?"

"Both, maybe?" Green asked aloud. "But mostly me."

Melissa slowed their steps to get a little distance from the rest of the group. "In that case, sure. What's up?"

Eight ideas ran for Green's mouth at once, blocking the exit and generally causing a metaphorical fire hazard. It wasn't just bleeding. It wasn't even just about bodies and curves and hair and hormone blockers and whether Melissa liked them, which was probably a rude way to start a conversation that Green had just said was about them, not her. It was also about nonbinary people who didn't make good best friends, and about boys who you liked so much you didn't know how to talk to them. Especially when they could look twenty feet ahead and see Ronnie laughing at something Rick said. His face sparkled when he laughed, like when a cartoon character smiles and a star appears on their front tooth with a little *ting*.

"You okay?" asked Melissa.

"Yeah." Green brought their eyes and attention back to the moment. "There's just a lot going on."

"I know the feeling." Melissa smiled and squeezed Green's hand.

Melissa's smile was the kind of smile that grownups said could light up a room. Green used to think that was a weird thing to say, but just then, it made the air feel a little less heavy. Green smiled too and waited for the thoughts in their head to slow down enough to figure out a place to begin. They looked away and there was Ronnie again, right in their line of sight.

"I think I like somebody," Green said.

"I like a lot of people!" said Melissa. "I like you, I like my mom, I like Kelly, I like Mx. Abrams . . ."

"Seriously? That has got to be the worst dad joke ever. Oh!" Green jumped back from their own words. "I mean, mom joke? I didn't mean to misgender you."

"Nah," said Melissa. "I think they're still dad jokes. Just be glad Kelly's not here."

Green laughed uncomfortably.

"What?" Melissa shrugged. "It's true. Sometimes the people who are trying to be helpful don't know when to stop. My mom's getting like that too, and well, it's a lot. I mean, it's way better than it was when my mom was tiptoeing around me like she might say *boo* and I'd turn into a lobster."

Green laughed, much more naturally this time.

"So you like someone," said Melissa. "That's cool."

"I don't know whether he likes me though. I don't even know if he likes people like me. He's straight." Green paused. "Well, not straight. But not *not* straight either."

Melissa wrinkled her nose. "What does that mean?"

"I don't know. He's the one who said he'd always liked girls *before*."

"Well, that sounds like he likes you."

"You think so?" Green asked hopefully.

"I do!" Melissa noticed the frown developing on Green's face. "So what's the problem?"

The fear that had been swirling in Green's head tumbled off their tongue. "If he's not willing to call himself queer, does he really see my gender?"

"Oh!" Melissa's eyes went wide. "That *is* a problem."

"Yeah." Green kicked at a rock on the sidewalk, and it bounced into the street.

"Well, I don't know about this kid, but I know Leila and I had to figure some stuff out at first."

"Really?" Green turned to Melissa in surprise.

"Yeah. She knew she was bisexual, but she hadn't dated a girl before, and then there was this *whole thing* where she was worried that I thought she was saying that maybe I wasn't a girl, which wasn't true at all, and we had to have a big talk about how it was okay to be unsure about what she thought but it wasn't okay to assume she was sure about what I thought."

"Wow, that sounds like a lot," said Green. It was comforting to know that they weren't the only one in a complicated situation. Maybe all relationships were complicated at some point or another.

"It all worked out. And it was worth it!" Melissa smiled. "I'll bet he's cute to cause all this trouble. I mean, everyone's cute in their own way, but this guy really must be something to have you all twisted up."

"Yeah." Green tried not to look Ronnie's way. When they failed, they tried not to linger on his cute face. They failed at that too, but if Melissa had noticed, she didn't say anything.

By then, Melissa's and Green's steps had slowed to a complete halt about half a block from the bus stop, outside of hearing range, especially for a crowd of boisterous middle school students. If Green was going to ask Melissa about hormone blockers, it was going to be now.

"If it were just that, though, I'd probably be okay. But then, this other thing happened."

And that's where Green halted again. First because they still didn't really like the word *period*, except that the other options were worse. Then because they remembered that Melissa wouldn't have periods, and maybe she didn't feel too great about that.

"And then?" Melissa said.

"Yeah," said Green. "And then."

"And then you stopped."

"Yeah, I did."

"Well, you don't have to keep going, but you can if you want to. I mean, I'm listening, and I'm real good with keeping things private. I have lots of practice."

"The thing is," Green whispered, "I got my period." A slick layer of shame washed over them. And then another wave of shame for having felt shame. Self-empowered nonbinary rock stars were supposed to feel good about their bodies. Only Green didn't feel so much like a rock star at the moment.

"Congratulations?" asked Melissa. "I mean, is it congratulations for you? Your face says maybe it's not congratulations."

Green sighed and shook their head. "I dunno."

"Bus is coming!" Ronnie yelled from the corner.

"I'll get the next one!" Melissa yelled back with a wave of her hand.

"You sure?" asked Green. They couldn't imagine passing up the chance to ride the bus with Ronnie. Of course, Melissa didn't have a crush on Ronnie, but Leila was taking the bus too. Maybe girlfriends were different from crushes.

Melissa nodded with a gleam in her eye.

"Thanks," said Green. "You sure you don't mind talking about this? I mean, your body doesn't—"

"I am well aware of my body," said Melissa firmly. "It's mine, so I try to love it." She grimaced a little bit as if to say that she didn't always succeed. "But I think I'm okay without bleeding every month."

Green picked mindlessly at the bark of a sidewalk maple tree until they realized they were doing it. They learned in third grade that it was bad for the tree, so they patted it a few times and said an internal *sorry, tree.* "So I know I said this was about me, but can I ask you a question?"

"As long as I don't have to answer it if I don't want to." That was Rainbow Spectrum's rule about questions, and Green thought it was a good one.

"Of course not. So my question, which you don't have to answer, is: You're on blockers, right?"

Melissa nodded. It wasn't something she talked about a lot, but she *had* told them about it. Her doctor prescribed hormone blockers to keep her body from making lots of testosterone and going through puberty.

"How did you decide to take them?"

"That sounds like a mirror question."

"A what?"

"That's what my therapist calls it when I ask her a question that maybe I should be asking myself. For me, hormone blockers were barely a decision at all. It was more like asking me whether I wanted to be able to breathe. But for you, it sounds like a tougher call."

"It is."

"It's not a race," said Melissa. "That one's from my therapist too."

"I don't think I need more time," said Green. "I don't want to decide more slowly. I just wish it wasn't an issue, like I didn't have to decide at all. I want to be a Mx. Potato Head, and put on whatever eyes and feet I want, and change them when I don't like them anymore."

"Yeeeah," said Melissa, drawing out the word. "That's not how bodies work."

"Tell me about it," said Green. "Sometimes gender

feels like a pop quiz I have to take every day . . . and I've never studied. I don't even know where the textbook is. Binary people have it so easy."

"It's not easy being a girl, even if you're cisgender!"

"True," said Green. "But you're a girl every day, right?"

"Yup!" Melissa beamed.

"Lucky," said Green.

"You could be a girl every day, too, if you wanted," Melissa offered, then batted her eyes to signal her sarcasm.

"Yeah," said Green. "Tried that. Failed. Definitely not a girl." Even the word made Green's tongue curl, when they used it for themself.

"One good thing about hormone blockers is that they're temporary," said Melissa. "So if you do change your mind, you just stop taking them, and everything in your body starts up again."

"Yeah, I read that," said Green.

"You don't sound excited," said Melissa.

"I . . . I don't think I am." Green startled at their own honesty.

"Then don't get hormone blockers." Melissa's words were simple, but they launched deep into Green's gut.

"But what if something happens and I change my mind?" Green said.

"Then you change your mind," said Melissa.

"Oh." It sounded so easy when Melissa said it. And so true.

"But also, I think the biggest thing already happened." Melissa tipped her head to the side. "You know . . ."

Green knew. Getting their period was a pretty big thing. But as gross and as weird as it felt, it was still their body and they didn't hate it. Yeah, it was changing, but so were they. And the lines between what was queer and what wasn't were getting fuzzier than ever.

"How are you so smart?"

Melissa shrugged. "Good luck? And therapy. But neither of those has made my social studies grade any better, so it's not everything."

"I'm glad blockers are the right thing for you," said Green. "But . . ." They paused and checked their body for alarm bells, but nothing felt off about what they were saying, so they continued. "I don't think they are for me. I'm gonna see how this body I'm in works for now."

"That's cool. Some bodies are right from the start. Others take a little customization."

"Is that another line from your therapist?" Green asked.

"Nah, that one's from my mom."

"Parents say the weirdest things."

"No kidding. Like, *clean your room!*" Melissa cheesed a giant grin.

"Or, *do your homework!*"

"Or, *I was there when you were born, so I know your gender!*"

By the time they stopped laughing, the next bus was visible a few blocks down, so Green walked with Melissa to the bus stop and waved as the bus pulled away.

It seemed weird that the choice to not do anything was such a big decision, but it was a decision Green was ready to make. Their body might not be everything they would create in an ideal body, and they might change it someday, but for now, they would see where the ride took them.

# ★ CHAPTER XVI ★

# FRIENDS OF DOROTHY

The week of the play, Jung Middle School buzzed with excitement. Signs advertising Wednesday evening's show were everywhere, and seeing them made Green feel proud to be part of the most exciting thing at school since the kitchen had introduced Muffin Mondays.

The biggest topic of conversation for the kids not in the production was who would be going to the show together. Lots of kids were going in groups, and a few of them took the opportunity to go in pairs and call it a date.

"Guess what?" said Devon at the Rainbow Spectrum lunch table on Tuesday.

"You saw a battle-axe-wielding troll running laps for gym class," exclaimed Melissa.

"And it squashed three kids on the way!" added Kelly.

"You always guess." Leila shook her head. "Why do you always guess?"

"It's a feature!" Melissa framed her face with her hands and grinned.

"So," asked Kelly, "what's the news?"

"I asked that boy from ballet class whether he would go to the show with me, and he said, *only if I would be his boyfriend!*"

"And?" asked Melissa.

"Now I have a date *and* a boyfriend."

The table broke out in cheers and applause until Devon's cheeks flushed and he waved his hands for them to stop.

"Congratulations!" said Rick. "Me, I'm bringing my family. I'm proud to show off how talented my friends are."

"So am I!" said Devon. "I'm just also proud to show off my new boyfriend *to* those talented friends."

Everyone laughed, but Green's laugh was mostly for show. They were only half paying attention to the conversation. Instead, they were wishing they had a date and a boyfriend too.

Things with Ronnie had gotten back to normal, on the surface anyway. Green was still giving Ronnie clementines, and he was still leaving them to the side until the end of lunchtime. Green had started to wonder whether it was because Ronnie didn't care about the clementines, or whether he cared about them very much and wanted to hang on to them as long as possible. But Green didn't know how to ask that. So instead, they kept bringing clementines and kept wondering what was going on in Ronnie's head.

Tuesday afternoon was dress rehearsal. That meant running through the whole play, start to finish, with the full cast, band, and crew. Victor, Kadyn, and Cindy were in charge of props and set changes, while Brinley and Violet went to the lighting booth with Ms. Jones.

Ronnie and Green took their places in the front row with scripts, just in case anyone forgot a line. They sat a seat apart—not close enough to touch without it being on purpose, but close enough for Green's nerves to vibrate.

The play opened on Melissa as Dorothy running after Toto, followed by a conversation with Dorothy's aunt and uncle about living someplace boring, and soon Melissa had launched into her big musical number, "Over the Rainbow."

To no one's surprise, Melissa was as great a vocalist as she was an actor, as she sang about a world with bluebirds above the chimney tops, and pondered why she couldn't be there too.

When Melissa was done, Green and Ronnie were the first to stand and clap as hard as they could. Ms. Jones, Mr. Sydney, and a few members of the cast started clapping too, and the rest joined in. Ronnie brought his fingers to his lips and whistled.

Green thought to themself that they'd love to learn how to whistle like that. Maybe they could ask Ronnie to teach them, which got them thinking about Ronnie's lips and how soft they must be. They felt their cheeks go warm and focused on clapping even harder.

When the applause faded, Mr. Sydney whispered to Ms. Jones and slipped out of the auditorium.

"Where's he going?" asked several members of the cast. Green wondered the same thing.

"That was beautiful, Melissa," said Ms. Jones. "But next time, no onstage applause. You are in the performance, not watching it. Mr. Sydney will be back with us in a bit. Now let's continue with the next scene."

When Mr. Sydney returned, his black-and-red-checkered bow tie was loose and his white sleeves had been rolled above his elbows. His eyes were red and puffy, and the base of his hair was wet, as if he had splashed water on his face. He had clearly been crying, but his grin didn't appear to be fake.

He took a seat a few seats down from Green and Ronnie, as the play continued. He stayed there until the end of the first act, when he approached the stage applauding and yelling, "You all look magnificent up there!"

Then he called the cast and crew into a circle, and the band turned to face the stage. Ms. Jones, Brinley, and Violet even came down from the lighting booth.

"I know, we're on a tight schedule this afternoon," said Mr. Sydney, a sure sign that he was about to make the schedule even tighter. "But please, indulge me as I say a few things before we get into Act II. If you came to Rainbow Spectrum last year, you probably have heard me say this, but I have grown so much with you kids. In fact, before last year, I might have let this moment go without a mention, but I wanted you to know, Melissa, you are amazing."

"It's not just me," Melissa said, and gestured around her.

Mr. Sydney stopped and held his thumb and forefinger tight to the bridge of his nose. "Okay, John, pull it together," he whispered to himself.

"Mr. Sydney," said Kelly, "if you're gonna cry every time Melissa does something amazing, you're gonna end up dehydrated."

Mr. Sydney laughed and brushed away a sniffle. "And you're right, Melissa, it's not just you. Do you know why Jung Middle School is still performing *The Wizard of Oz*?"

"Because the school system is underfunded?" Tracey smirked.

"It helps to have the scripts and costumes ready, sure," said Mr. Sydney. "But the storeroom is filled with costumes and sets from plays we're not putting on, and if there was really a need, we could look into raising the funds, like we did with the flying-pig costumes. But *The Wizard of Oz* is a tradition here, and with good reason. Did you ever stop to think what the play's about?"

"Sure," said Mika. "A stranger comes to town and kills witches."

Mr. Sydney laughed. "That's one take on it, sure, but it's a story about finding your people. Did you know that for a long time the QUILTBAG+ community considered *The Wizard of Oz* to be a queer allegory?"

"Because of 'Over the Rainbow'?" asked Tracey.

"In part," said Mr. Sydney. "Though the song is older than the rainbow flag."

The room filled with gasps, along with Leila saying, "That's right! Gilbert Baker created the flag in 1978."

"Crumpets and tea!" Mr. Sydney exclaimed, holding his hand to his chest. "When you put it that way, *I'm* older than the rainbow flag." He shook his head to dispel the image. "Anyway, Judy Garland was before my time, but she played Dorothy in the movie version of *The Wizard of Oz*, and was a huge gay icon."

"Judy Garland was gay?" cried Mika.

"No," said Mr. Sydney. "At least, I don't think so. But she starred in a movie that was all about how she couldn't be herself at home, at a time when most gay people weren't welcome to be themselves with their families. In fact, at a time when most people couldn't be out, a lot of men would signal that they were a *Friend of Dorothy* as a way to say that they were interested in other men."

"I can see it," said Talia. "Dorothy's stuck in this boring Kansas world, and she wants to go somewhere different. If I were the only gay guy I knew in Kansas, I might want to leave too."

"Exactly!" said Mr. Sydney. "Especially if you were worried that you might get beat up. Or worse," he said, shaking his head. "For a long time, Hollywood was one of the few places it was relatively safe to be gay. You still had to be careful, but Hollywood was built on secrets, and a lot of those secrets were about who was queer."

"Plenty of them still are," said Ms. Jones. "And while this is a rich conversation, we had better move on to Act II if any of you want to get home in time to finish your homework."

The students who had Ms. Jones for math groaned

the loudest. She never assigned less than ten prob-lems a night. Twenty if they were short.

"Thank you for the reminder, Ms. Jones. And thank you all for taking a moment to explore QUILTBAG+ history with me. I hope it gives some context for why we're still doing this silly old play."

"Well, I'm a Friend of Dorothy for sure!" said Melissa with a twirl.

"Me too!" said Mika and Talia simultaneously.

"Count me in!" said Green.

"I'm a *Girlfriend* of Dorothy!" said Leila, wrapping her arms around Melissa and giving her a kiss on the cheek.

"Okay, you fabulous Friends of Dorothy, let's get to Act II," said Mr. Sydney. "And I promise no more soliloquies from me. At least, not today."

Green and Ronnie went back to sitting in the audience with their scripts, just a seat apart. Green thought about people who couldn't say that they were queer, not because they didn't know, but because it wasn't safe. They had to hide whether they wanted to or not. Green wondered what people who weren't sure whether they were queer did if they didn't have a safe place to ask questions and try out possibilities. Probably nothing. They probably never got to explore who they really were.

When Green thought about it that way, what people called themselves mattered a whole lot less than who they wanted to spend time with, and Green wanted to spend time with Ronnie. They hoped that after the play was over, Ronnie would still want to spend time with them too.

# CHAPTER XVII

# GREEN REACHES EMERALD CITY

Ms. Han and the band warmed up while Ms. Jones and the crew took tickets and helped people find their seats. Even with the same tile walls and old posters, the auditorium felt like a real theater as the seats filled with families and friends holding their coats and playbills in their laps.

"Hey, Green!"

Green turned around to see Rick smiling. Three adults stood behind him. A tall man wore a dark pantsuit and had his arm around a rounder woman in a similarly dark skirt suit. Next to them, an older man with white hair wore a soft red sweater and blue jeans, with pointy red nails.

"These are my parents," said Rick. "And this is my grandpa, Gamma Ray!"

"Nice to meet you," said Green. "Nice name, Gamma Ray!"

"Thank you," he said, firing an imaginary laser into the air. *"Pew pew!"*

Green found their own dad already seated next to Kelly's. The two of them were deep in a conversation about Metallica bass lines. Lulu, Jan, Kandy, Randey, and River were nearby. Or at least Lulu and Jan were nearby. Kandy, Randey, and River were running between the rows of seats and meowing at strangers, pretending they were cats.

Nana was there, too, sitting up front, close to where the American Sign Language interpreters would stand. She was chatting with Mika's parents, who were also Deaf.

Melissa's mom and Scott sat near the front, too, with a large bouquet of pink carnations sticking out of a bag between them, to be given to Melissa after the show.

"Mx. Abrams!" Green called when they saw the Rainbow Spectrum advisor, and made their way over. "Did you bring Max?!"

"Sorry, Green. Max is still too young for theater. But I did bring my partner, Tim."

A tall, blond man wearing a T-shirt with cartoon dinosaurs in a band held out his hand. "Pleasure to meet you."

Green saw Mama B and Mama C pulling Ronnie into a hug. He only looked slightly embarrassed by it; he still had that special smile that went all the way up to his eyes.

Jay was there with a few other kids, including Tracey, until Ms. Jones noticed her and told her to get backstage immediately. She wasn't in costume yet.

"But I'm not in the first three scenes," she protested. "I can change then!"

"Go!" said Ms. Jones. "Before Mr. Sydney panics."

"He knows I'm here."

"TRACEY!"

"I think you'd better go," said Jay.

"It's fine," said Tracey, but she got up and ran backstage.

When Minh, Mr. Sydney's partner, arrived, Green showed him to the special seat in the front row that had been roped off with yellow yarn for him.

"I think this is the first performance of John's that I haven't been pressed into helping out at some point," said Minh. "It's pretty exciting to be in the audience."

"Enjoy the show!" said Green.

Once the audience was mostly seated, Ms. Jones sent Ronnie, Green, Kadyn, Cindy, and Victor backstage, while she went to the lighting booth with Brinley and Violet.

Mr. Sydney had already gathered the cast into a large circle that shifted to make room. Ronnie stood next to Green, their sneakers touching.

"Alright, thespians," said Mr. Sydney, wearing a black button-down shirt with a gold-trimmed rainbow bow tie. "Let's get ready to show this audience what you've got!"

"'Thespians'?" asked Dini, dressed in a sparkly white suit with green trim as the Wizard of Oz. "Like lesbians after they burn their tongues?"

Even Mr. Sydney laughed. "No, and it doesn't stand for theater lesbians either. At least, not officially."

"He means actors." Tracey held up her phone, with the definition on the screen. She was wearing her witch dress, but she was still in her sneakers.

"Tracey!" cried Mr. Sydney. "You have your phone

on you?! What if someone calls you while you're onstage?"

"What if I need to take a picture?" Tracey retorted. "It's on silent. It's not like people use their phones to make calls anyway."

"Regardless, I don't need you getting distracted with other creative pursuits and suddenly our Wicked Witch has disappeared before the scene where Dorothy gets her."

Melissa tossed an imaginary bucket of water at Tracey, who flailed her arms over her head as she mimed melting into a pool of nothing.

"You can goof all you want in two hours. For now, focus your thoughts on the performance."

"Sorry, Mr. Sydney." Tracey dropped her phone into her backpack and tossed the bag backstage.

Mr. Sydney gave a brief speech about the wonder of the stage as a place to explore your own life by exploring someone else's and to engage in the vast array of human experience. For the most part, the cast was confused, but they knew what he meant when he said that he was honored to have been their director, and they knew that he said *break a leg* because the theater was full of superstitions.

The band started to play. Near the end of the overture, Melissa took her first mark, dressed in a blue gingham dress, her hair in two braids. She held a stuffed dog under her arm. Everyone else watched quietly from the wings of the stage, except for Green and Ronnie.

They stood on either side of the thick rope that ran up the side of the stage. Their cue was the overture's final crescendo. It was possible for one person to open the heavy stage curtains, but four hands pulling meant the curtain opened more smoothly. It was also possible for them to put four hands on the rope without touching, but as they pulled, their hands brushed against each other, tickling both Green's thumbs and their heart.

With that, Act I had begun. Green and Ronnie sat right next to each other leaning against the backstage wall, following along with the script in case anyone forgot a line.

Act I went fabulously, and no one needed a line prompt. Melissa was charming, and the band played beautifully. It was the same show Green had seen dozens of times in bits and pieces, but rarely as a whole, and never with the accents of an audience's responses. Green watched the people watching the play more than the performance itself, waiting for them to laugh when a joke was coming up, noticing when someone spotted their kid in the chorus. More than a few people cried when Melissa sang "Over the Rainbow." Mr. Sydney wiped his eyes more than once too.

Melissa made her way to Oz, and once she had met up with her journey partners, it was time for Green and Ronnie to lower the curtain to signal the end of the first act.

Intermission was only ten minutes long, so Mr. Sydney told the cast and crew to stay backstage unless they really needed to use the bathroom, and even then, they should cut the line.

Green was glad they didn't have to go. The private nurse's stall they used was on the other side of the building, and it would have been tough to get back in time for Act II. They could have asked someone else on the crew to fill in, but there were only four chances to lift and lower the curtain along with Ronnie, and they didn't want to miss a single one.

The hum of hundreds of voices on the other side of the curtain grew louder for a moment, and then someone was tackle-hugging Melissa.

"You were great!" Kelly exclaimed, dressed in

a white shirt, black pants, and sequined emerald green vest, like the rest of the band.

"She *is* great!" responded Leila. "Or at least, she will be, if you don't break her leg!"

"I mean, this is the the-*ay*-ter!" Kelly gestured grandly around her. "Isn't that the thing to do here?"

"Kelly!" Ms. Sydney cried. "What are you doing back here?"

"It's intermission." Kelly shrugged.

The tall kid who played bassoon popped his head backstage next, and soon half the band was there, along with Ms. Han, who was wondering where her musicians had gone.

"At least they're here, instead of out in the audience," Ms. Han said.

"True," Mr. Sydney replied. "Trying to wrest them back from their families would have been a nightmare!"

While the cast and band gabbed, the crew prepared the stage for Act II. Kadyn pulled the ropes that lowered the Emerald City/Witch's Castle backdrop, while Victor and Cindy wheeled out the bright green door with a circle cutout that represented the gates of Emerald City and aligned it with tape marks on the floor.

Green's eyes were on the clock. So were Ronnie's. Perhaps even more important than raising the curtain, it was their job to flicker the lights twice when only two minutes remained in the intermission, and again when there were thirty seconds, to remind the audience to take their seats and for the cast and band to be ready to perform.

Green took the blocky black switch on the left and Ronnie took the one on the right. They counted down from three, and with a heavy *chunk-ca-chunk*, they flashed the lights.

Green and Ronnie opened the curtain again for the start of Act II, hand over hand, lingering for a few moments after the actors had begun.

The first scene of Act II went great. So did the start of the second.

That's when Tracey screamed.

Mr. Sydney's head whipped in her direction. "Tracey!" he whispered. "What happened?"

"I left something when I went to the bathroom!"

"Whatever it is, I'm sure it will still be there later. You can get it then."

"It's my hat!" Tracey whisper-yelled, smacking her bare head with her palm. "My witch's hat!"

Mr. Sydney looked like he was about to say something, but bit his lip instead.

"I'll get it!" Kadyn dashed off to the bathroom.

"I'll go with her!" Cindy followed her down the stage steps and along the side of the auditorium, the sounds of their footsteps echoing as they ran.

"I guess I'll stay here and handle the props," said Victor.

Mr. Sydney told everyone to remain calm, but he loosened his bow tie and kept twirling his hair between his fingers. Dini paced back and forth, and Tracey bounced in place. Ronnie and Green looked at each other nervously.

Kadyn and Cindy returned out of breath and empty-handed at the start of scene three.

"It wasn't there!" Cindy exclaimed.

"Someone must have taken it!" Tracey cried.

"Or maybe you left it in the audience when you were hanging out with your friends!" said Kadyn.

Mr. Sydney massaged the bridge of his nose with his forefingers. "I told you to come right back," he said, as though to himself.

"I'll go check the audience!" Tracey said, but Dini stopped her.

"Tracey! You can't go anywhere. You're in the next scene!"

"We'll go!" Ronnie announced, jumping up and putting out his hand to Green to haul them up too.

It was dark in the audience, and Green and Ronnie had to wait a few seconds for their eyes to adjust so they didn't bang into anyone. They stood side by side, Green's heart thumping so loud in their rib cage they were sure Ronnie could hear it.

Once they could see, they made their way down the aisle, their eyes looking out for a pointy black hat. Well, a pointy hat, anyway, since everything was shades of gray and black beyond the bright stage, where Dini's Wizard of Oz voice boomed from his onstage hideout.

The stage lights went on and off again, and scene four began. The very next scene was at the Wicked Witch's castle.

"Oh no! I see it!" Ronnie whispered.

"Isn't that a good thing?" Green whispered back.

Ronnie tsked. "Some kid is wearing it. I'm not good with kids."

"I am! Point 'em out to me!"

Ronnie lined his face up near Green's and pointed to the far side of the theater. Green almost hoped they wouldn't find the kid right away, so that Ronnie would have to press up closer and try again, but Green spotted the hat immediately. And the kid wasn't just any kid.

"That's River!" Green said, a little louder than they meant to, and several of the adults near them turned their way with disapproving faces. "I'll be right back!" they said more quietly, and ran over.

"Hi, Green!" Kandy and Randey shouted before Green could motion for them to stay quiet, and more adults gave disapproving looks.

"If you three don't keep it down," Lulu hissed, then noticed Green behind her.

"Hey! Show's going great." She flashed two thumbs-ups.

"Thanks," said Green, "But it won't be great if I don't get back that hat from River."

"What ha—?" Lulu's eyes went wide. "How in the world—? How did I not see—?"

Green didn't have time for Lulu to keep starting questions and not finishing them.

"River," they said, as calmly as they could manage. "Where did you get that hat?"

"The witch let me wear it," River said proudly.

"Well, the witch needs it back."

"She didn't ask for it back."

"Yeah, well, I am," Green said.

River considered that, as Dorothy and her new friends onstage decided to head to the witch's castle. Green looked back at Ronnie, whose face was in a panic. They held up a finger to say, *just one more minute.*

"You know," said Green. "I wouldn't make a witch mad."

"She isn't a real witch," River said confidently. "She's just a kid playing a witch."

"Okay, you're right," said Green. "She's just a kid playing a witch. And how silly would she look onstage without the right hat?"

"Oh." River understood the importance of a good costume. Without another word, they pulled the hat off their head and handed it over.

"Thanks, buddy!" said Green. "You're a great kid!"

Green ran backstage, waving the hat in their hand, with Ronnie right behind them. They handed the hat off to Tracey who popped it on her head just in time to head onstage.

"We did it!" said Green, flopping against the backstage wall.

"*You* did it!" said Ronnie, flopping near them and letting his arm rest against Green's.

Some people laughed when the flying pigs came out, and a few people cheered, but Green was too busy being next to Ronnie to notice.

Before long, Melissa had thrown the bucket full of blue confetti that was supposed to represent water on Tracey, who flailed dramatically and crumpled to the floor. Dini, as the Wizard, gave them each their awards, and Melissa clicked her heels to go home.

The band played the final number as the cast came back out to wild applause, starting with the chorus. Then the people with smaller speaking roles came out, followed by the Cowardly Lion, the Tin Queer, the Scarecrow, the witches, and, finally, Melissa as Dorothy. They pointed backstage to represent the crew, and to the band below them. The cast linked together for one final bow. And then in a move not even Mr. Sydney had been prepared for, they all curtsied. The room overflowed with applause, cheers, whistles, and people yelling things like, "That's my baby!" and "Go, Melissa!"

The cast put their costumes into a big bag to be washed and used again in a few years and ran out to the audience while the crew gathered the props.

"You coming to the after-party?" Leila asked Green, once the backstage had mostly cleared out. Leila lived a few blocks away, and her mom had let her invite over the entire cast, crew, and band for pizza.

"Yup!" said Green.

"You know it!" said Ronnie, who was next to them.

They all stood quietly for a moment. Leila looked at Green, over at Ronnie, and back to Green. "Oh," she said with a smile, and disappeared.

Then it was just Green and Ronnie backstage.

Ronnie took a deep breath, but instead of talking, he let it out in a big *whoosh*ing sigh. Then he did it again, and a third time.

"What are you doing?" asked Green.

"It's a thing my moms do. It's about moving the energy around so the words can come out freely. It sounds silly, but it really works. Well, usually it does." He took another deep breath and *whoosh*ed again.

"Do you want to go out sometime?" Green asked. "Not to the party. That too. But some other time, just us."

"Like, on a date?" Ronnie's eyes got big.

"Yes? I mean, if you want to."

Ronnie's silence was uncomfortably long. Green grew nervous that they had misunderstood what Ronnie wanted to say between all that whooshing, that they had misunderstood their hands touching on the curtain rope, that they had misunderstood most of the last two months.

Eventually Ronnie uttered a quiet "but . . ." that trailed off into nothing.

Green's stomach flopped. "But?"

"But what if you're the only nongirl I ever like?"

"Hold on!" said Green. "Did you just basically say you like me?"

"I do like you, Green Gibson."

"And I like you, Ronnie Lewis."

Green leaned in toward Ronnie.

Ronnie leaned in toward Green.

Their noses were six inches apart. Then three. Then one.

Green thought Ronnie's lips touched theirs first, but later, Ronnie swore that it was Green who had started it. Soft on soft, warm on warm, brief and light as a breeze, they kissed.

"Can we do that again?" asked Ronnie, so close Green could feel Ronnie's breath on their lips.

"Yes, please," said Green, trying to keep a goofy smile under control.

They kissed a second time, and then a third, each light peck a moment of what was to come. And what was to come was so much more than either of them could ever have imagined.

# ★ ACKNOWLEDGMENTS ★

No writer is an island, not even one who has a home of one's own. This is the fifth time I've had the privilege to write a book's acknowledgments, and the fifth time I will fail to adequately express my love and appreciation for everyone who has helped me and my writing. And yet, I persevere through imperfection like some sort of life lesson.

Ever thanks to my parents, Cindy and Steve Gino, who have supported my storytelling from before I could write by transcribing my stories and telling their own. (*The Adventures of Cupcake and Donut Forever!*) Robin Gridgeman, I'm so glad to know you as an adult. Sorry I made you and your friends taste vanilla extract. Kadyn and Brinley Gridgeman, you are the best niblets an uncle could hope for, and I'm excited to see you grow up.

Miss Holly Hessinger, you bring a special light to my life. And Mike Jung, you inspire me every time we talk. I'm lucky to know you both.

Deep appreciation for my editor, David Levithan, who sees past what I wrote to what I could be saying; designer Maeve Norton who gives a thousand reasons to judge a book by its cover; and everyone at Scholastic who promotes my stories and helps get them into kids' hands. Countless gratitude for my agent Jenn Laughran, who never fails to tell it like it is.

Thank-yous galore to young readers of early versions of *Green*: Oliver O'Neal, Julia Powlus, Nicole Robbins, Sophie Esterly, Charlotte Smith, and Iris LaMastro, as well as grown-up readers Timnah Steinman, Beth Kelly, Kyle Lukoff, Jen Herrington, and Ingrid Conley-Abrams. Your feedback made this book what it is. Special thanks to Jasper Carney and Kate Tanner, who named twins Kandy and Randey in connection with a donation to We Need Diverse Books.

Regard beyond measure for the librarians and educators who have supported LGBTQIA+ stories and creators, especially in this current book panic. You are doing the impossibly hard work every day that makes my dream career possible.

When I wrote the acknowledgments for my first book, *Melissa*, not a single middle grade book with a transgender main character had been released by a major publisher. Now, eight years later, there are so many books for young people with trans characters that I don't even know what they all are, much less have I read them. And more and more stories about queer and trans communities are coming from within queer and trans communities! I have peers! Yay, peers! Let's keep writing great stories!

Finally, to you, great thanks for taking in my words. I hope you get a fraction of the joy and love from reading them that I did in writing them for you. Sparkle on!

# ★ ABOUT THE AUTHOR ★

**Alex Gino** is the author of the middle grade novels *Alice Austen Lived Here*; *Rick*; *You Don't Know Everything, Jilly P!*; and the Stonewall Award–winning *Melissa*. They love glitter, ice cream, gardening, awe-ful puns, and stories that reflect the complexity of being alive. For more information, visit alexgino.com.